Brittany

May your life
be filled with
love and happiness!
Love Taylor

Oreo the Miracle Dog

Saint Oreo
The Miracle Dog

By
Louis E. Tagliaferri

Other Novels by the Author

Bellaria di Rivergaro

The Web Shop

The Habsburg Cowboys

In Search of Becca

The Timucuan

Cracker Landing

Independently published 2019
by Louis E. Tagliaferri
Ponte Vedra, Florida 32081
Contact: loutag38@gmail.com

Printed in the United States of America

Library of Congress

ISBN – 13: 9781689349604

Dedication

This book is dedicated to our little Shih Tzu, Oreo, whose funny antics, unconditional love and companionship continue to brighten our lives and were the inspiration for this story.

Prologue

On his last birthday, his forty-fourth, the bearded man wearing the robe of a friar had been quite ill. However, that was an eternity ago and now he strode confidently across the field of rolling, green grass that rippled from a light wind blowing over it. The sky was the most vivid blue imaginable and was dotted by pure white, fluffy clouds drifting lazily across the scene below. Ahead of him was a small stream fed from snowmelt in the picturesque mountains to the west. He could hear the murmur of crystal clear water flowing over ancient glacial rocks as he approached a place where the stream pooled and animals gathered to quench their thirst. It was a perfect day. How could it not be?

Accompanying him on his purposeful walk were several farm animals, including a mule, a few sheep and a lamb or two. Birds that had been nesting in the forest just beyond the stream came out to greet him, while curious squirrels and rabbits cautiously gathered to see who was coming. He was loved by all of them. However, the smaller creatures were held at bay by the incessant barking of a small brown and white dog that was taking charge of clearing the area so its master would not be bothered by what it playfully considered the "riff raff."

"Ah, so there you are," the man said. "I have a feeling you knew I was looking for you." As he spoke, the dog stopped barking and bounded over to him, leaping into his arms. It was as though it had been a long time

1

since the man and dog had been together and now they were having a joyful reunion; although in this timeless place they had never really been apart.

"Well, now, young pup. I have a job for you," the man said to the squirming animal. He knew that in its own way the creature understood exactly what was being said. There had always been a special bond between the two of them.

The man carried the dog back a little way toward the open field and put him down. "It won't take you very long," he said. "You will be back very soon and I will love you even more for what you are going to do."

He petted the dog once more and pointed toward the field. "Be off with you now! You know where to go."

The dog gave the man a mournful look as though it were saying, "Why me? I really don't want to go." But, the man simply smiled and motioned for the dog to scoot away. Then, the animal turned and bounded across the field to go where it was needed.

"That was an excellent choice," a voice behind the man said. There was a flutter of excitement among all of the animals as the words were spoken. Even the sound of the wind and the bubbling stream seemed to take on a new, more respectful tone.

Turning around to face the speaker, the man said, "Yes, he will do fine. And, thank you for approving my request."

"How could I not? They truly need help. By the way, did you give him a name?"

"I did," the man said. "They will call him Oreo."

Chapter One

Melinda Taltson was perplexed as she sat at her desk in the Hanford Metro Women's Shelter not far from the Illinois state capitol. She listened attentively to Brenda Hopkins, who once again turned down Melinda's offer to move into the shelter where she could obtain the medical assistance and job skills training she needed. Brenda was one of the city's 175 chronic homeless people. Although she was a regular food recipient of the shelter and, at least once every week or so, made use of its public shower facilities, Brenda lived with more than two dozen other male and female homeless people, who she called her family. The group lived in a controversial camping tent complex adjacent to the downtown park. The tent complex was pejoratively called Hanford Heights by downtown residents and the hundreds of people who commuted to the city daily to work in its shops and offices.

Hanford Heights was only one of the city's homeless complexes. Like the others, it consisted of tents, homemade lean-to's, tarps draped over large beach umbrellas and just about anything else that could provide inhabitants with some privacy and protection from the elements. Brenda began her life as a homeless person at age sixteen. Her alcoholic mother stabbed her live-in boyfriend when she caught him trying to rape Brenda. Brenda ran out of the tenement screaming and never returned. That night she wandered past a group of homeless people who had been camping under a flyover ramp just outside the downtown area. An older woman who was roasting a chicken over a fire in a makeshift grill spotted her and said,

"You just done run away, now didn't you girl?"

Brenda simply nodded her head. Then the woman said, "I be Alicia. You look hungry. Come on over and have a bit of this here chicken. Then you best be think'n about where you gonna sleep tonight. Gonna be cold, I think."

For the next three months, Brenda stayed with Alicia who introduced her to Horace, Mamma Louise, Angelina, Billy Joe and the other homeless people in the camp.

"You stay by us. We teach you all you need to know," Alicia told her.

Brenda learned where the safe places in the city were and which areas she should avoid – the drug infested ones in particular. Hard drugs, that is, because practically everyone in the camp was on something less potent. She learned where to go to get the best free meals, free clothing and hot showers; the latter being a periodic necessity. At the shelters, she quickly found out which counselors were decent and sincere and which couldn't really give a damn about their clients' well-being. She learned which cops were nice and which just wanted a little "snatch," especially from a good-looking young girl.

Of course, there was a downside to living in the camp. At times, life there could be violent. Brenda was raped twice and became pregnant once. She lost the child in the fourth month because of lack of proper pre-natal care. Then, one day the police descended in mass on the camp and forced all of the homeless to evacuate the area. The camp's residents scattered, in some cases being forced to leave behind the only possessions they had in the world. Brenda and Alicia took refuge at the Hanford Metro Women's Shelter. That is where Brenda met Melinda Taltson, a counselor to the homeless.

"Brenda, you are a very intelligent young woman," Melinda said. "All of your test scores are in the upper twenty-fifth percentile. You show particular aptitude for dealing with data, which suggests that you might be quite successful in a coding job or one that requires similar skill sets."

As Melinda was speaking, Brenda avoided her glance and just looked down at the floor. "Wouldn't you rather stay here at the shelter and let us help you?"

Brenda shook her head. "Not now, ma'am. But thank you."

Melinda did her best to hide her frustration. It was such a challenge trying to help the homeless – most who did not want to help themselves. The resistance to public assistance was somewhat understandable among the twenty to twenty-five percent of the homeless who were mentally ill. Processing information rationally and then making rational decisions was difficult if not impossible for many of them. Those unfortunate men and women were suffering from depression, anxiety, bipolar disorder, schizophrenia and psychosis, to name only a few disorders. A larger percentage of the homeless were alcoholics or were addicted to drugs ranging from meth and cocaine to heroin and prescription drugs. However, Melinda knew that Brenda did not fit into any of those categories, albeit like so many of the homeless she was a frequent cannabis user.

Not willing to write off her client, Melinda asked Brenda another question, fully anticipating the response since she had asked Brenda the same question on other occasions.

"Brenda, I respect you as an individual and I respect your right to live your life as you choose. However, could you please help me understand what has attracted you so much to Hanford Heights?"

Brenda looked up at Melinda quizzically. "It's because they are my friends," she said, as though the reason should be obvious to everyone. "They are the only friends I have. I can't leave them. They need me and I need them."

Melinda sighed. "Well then, at least know that you are welcome here anytime. So are the other women at the Heights."

Brenda nodded again and simply said, "Thank you, ma'am."

"Don't forget to stop at the pantry on your way out," Melinda said as she rose from her chair. "By the way, how is the tent you got from the church working out?"

"Just fine, ma'am. I'm snug and cozy in it. I like it just fine."

After Brenda left the shelter, Melinda remained at her desk making notes and completing the client interview report on her laptop. She stopped in the middle of a paragraph and sat back in her chair with her eyes closed. A voice from the doorway interrupted her thoughts.

"It doesn't get any easier, does it?" asked Rachael Owens, Melinda's supervisor.

"No," Melinda said swiveling her chair around to face Rachael. "This one, however, breaks my heart. That girl has a lot of potential. If anything, she should be sitting here in this office helping clients rather than being where she is on the other end."

"How old is she?"

"She just turned nineteen. She has been living in homeless camps for over two years and just can't seem to be able to break out of that life style."

Rachael agreed. "It is a pity. We have so much to offer women like her here. Why didn't Child Protective Services pick her up while she was still a minor?"

"She hid from them. The homeless, you know, protect their own. Her mother almost killed her live-in boyfriend and is serving 5 to 10 at the Travis Correctional Facility outside the city. No father, no known living relatives, no one wants her, except her "friends" at the Heights or where ever else they decide to set up camp."

"It seems like it will take something extraordinary to break her out of that mold," Rachael said.

"Yeah. A little miracle would do just fine," Melinda replied, her eyes pleading as she turned them upward toward the ceiling.

Brenda neatly placed the four paper bags filled with dry and canned goods she was given at the shelter's pantry into a rusted grocery cart. It was getting late and she wanted to get back to the Heights while there was still plenty of daylight. She kicked the hub of the cart's left rear wheel to make sure it was secure and then pushed the cart along the sidewalk toward Hanford Heights ten blocks away. She quickened her pace as she passed through a three-block area known as the "Gutter," which was where the hard-core addicts shot up and traded really bad stuff like heroin laced with fentanyl. Along the way, she had to step around several male and female addicts shooting up or laying passed out, covered in their own filth. At least the Heights is a lot better than this, she thought. For the most part, we clean up our own mess so that it almost looks like a real campground, she thought, remembering the time when she was twelve years old and went on a camping trip with the church youth group.

Hanford Park, where the homeless camp had been set up after the police evicted the group from their previous camp, was in the north central part of the city. It occupied two square blocks of prime downtown real estate lining up on a north-south direction dividing Main Street into two halves. Southbound traffic flowed along the park's west side while the opposite was true for northbound traffic. Large Victorian and Antebellum houses adorned the west side of the park while twelve to fifteen story high-rise office buildings rose on the opposite east side. A commercial area of lesser quality bled southward from the park and led into a typical urban area that included the Hanford Metro Women's Shelter. Only a few short blocks northbound from the park, the urban area quickly blended into the rural countryside.

When Brenda's group of homeless people were kicked out of the flyover area, they made their way to Hanford Park where they set up camp in the park's southeast quadrant, opposite the high-rise office buildings. That lasted three days before occupants of the office buildings complained to the police pointing out that overnight camping of any type was not permitted in the park. However, thanks to the advice of a sympathetic ACLU attorney, the homeless group learned that there was no such prohibition governing the sidewalks bordering the park. So, the homeless simply moved their tents and shelters onto the sidewalks where there was absolutely nothing the city could do about it. Nonetheless, most of the people who lived or worked in Hanford were appalled by the homeless complex. The problem was they did nothing about it except complain.

Seeing Brenda coming toward them with a shopping cart filled with groceries, several residents of the Heights greeted her expectantly.

A woman named Rosario, who had a very weathered face, hollered, "Hey there Brenda! What you got for us today?" By the time Brenda reached her tent, more than a half-dozen of her neighbors had gathered waiting for her.

"I got lots of good stuff from the pantry," Brenda answered. "Cans of peanut butter, baked beans, corn, beets and green beans. There are also a few boxes of crackers and cereal. They also gave me powdered milk for the cereal. Don't need any sugar cause the cereal is sweet all by itself. Got some Oreo cookies, though. And, there are a few gallon bottles of spring water on the bottom rack of the cart!"

"Honey, you the one who done made the trip to the shelter. So, take what you want first and then we be divvying up what's left," Mamma Louise told her.

Brenda laughed. She told everybody that she had already picked out what she wanted, including the Oreo cookies that she promised to share with them. Picking up one of the paper bags, she opened the fly of her tent and went inside. Miss Melinda would be surprised and pleased if she could see how neatly I arranged everything, Brenda thought.

Brenda got the tent from the Mission Church down the street. She just happened to be passing by the church on the day they were giving away donated items to the poor and homeless in the neighborhood. The tent had obviously seen better days. Nonetheless, although worn, it was quite serviceable and it was fully large enough for her. The base of the tent measured 8' X 6' and its center height was almost five feet. It was one of the easy setup kind with a wide entrance flap and three zippered, screened window flaps. Brenda was a petite 5' 1" so she could almost stand up fully erect in the tent and needed only a slight stoop to comfortably enter or exit it.

Inside the tent, there was a full-size air mattress with fitted sheets, a pillow and blankets, an orange crate cabinet with two shelves for storing groceries, several stacked plastic storage bins that held clothes and personal items and an old metal folding chair. On top of the cabinet were a comb, hair brush, tooth brush and paste, a mirror, bible and a homemade wash basin that Brenda formed by using a pair of scissors to cut a gallon plastic water bottle in half. Next to the air mattress, on the floor of the tent, were some stuffed animals including a teddy bear, lamb, kitten and a little dog; all representing the pets she never had as a child. Next to those was a plastic bucket that Brenda used when she needed to relieve herself during the night. Lastly, hanging from the top center of the tent was an LED lantern.

That night, most of the residents of Hanford Heights participated in a communal evening meal, as they frequently did when the weather was good. Very few of the homeless people in the Heights went to bed hungry. There were many sources of free food available to them and when anyone was in need, food was readily shared by everyone. The problem was nutrition. Although there was a relative abundance of canned and packaged food, none of the residents had refrigeration. There was no way to preserve fresh vegetables or fruit or any of the canned food once opened. Therefore, many of the residents suffered from nutritional deficiencies which, in turn, led to various diseases including painful periodontal disease and loss of teeth. Brenda was one of the few residents of the Heights to take advantage of clinical medical services at the Metro Women's Shelter. In addition, her personal hygienic practices were much better than most of her neighbors. Therefore, she was among the healthiest of the Height's residents.

After a light, but tasty, meal and some good-natured banter with her neighbors, Brenda decided to retire for the night. She turned on the LED lantern, zipped up the tent entrance flap and laid down on her air mattress. She read a few passages from the bible then turned out the lantern and tried to go to sleep. As usual, the noise of cars driving past the cluster of tents and makeshift shelters would be troublesome until about 11:00 pm. Next, she reached over, grabbed the stuffed dog and clutched it to her breast, crying softly to herself. She knew that she had to find a better life for herself, but how to do this completely escaped her. Finally, she drifted off to sleep, dreaming that she was a little girl playing with the puppy she always wanted but never had.

Chapter Two

The rain began a little after two o'clock in the morning. At first, it was a light drizzle; then it came down much heavier. The noise of the rain beating against the tent woke Brenda. She jumped up and turned on the LED lantern, checking to make sure that nothing in the tent touched the tent walls. She knew that if something like a sleeping bag was touching the side of a tent during the rain, it would serve much like a wick and soak up water.

After assuring herself the tent was secure from the rain, Brenda laid down again on the air mattress and tried going back to sleep. However, she was startled by something clawing at the side of the tent next to her air mattress. Whatever it was whined and scratched so violently that Brenda was sure it would claw its way into the tent. A large rat, she thought! There are plenty of those around the camp. Or maybe it was a raccoon or even something larger trying to find food. She was terrified. But then, the whine turned into a bark and the creature moved from the side of the tent to the front.

Mustering up courage, Brenda unzipped just enough of the tent flap so she could peek outside. She found herself looking at the face of a drenched brown and white dog that was clearly begging to get out of the rain. Without thinking further, Brenda unzipped the front flap, trying her best to keep the rain from coming into the tent. As soon as the dog saw the gap in the flap it jumped inside, shook itself violently to shed as much of the rainwater as possible and sat down looking at Brenda with the most pitiful but compelling brown eyes she had ever seen. "You poor little creature," Brenda said softly. Then she grabbed a towel that had been lying in a corner of the tent and began wiping the dog's fur. Before long, the hapless animal was reasonably dry.

Brenda had no idea where the dog came from or what to do with it; except it would be heartless to send it back out into the rain. For its own part, the dog seemed very content to simply sit on the tent floor as it looked at Brenda with gratitude. Then, it stood up, stretched and jumped on Brenda's ruffled bedding, snuggling itself at the bottom facing the entrance flap as though to guard against intruders.

Oh my God, what do I do with this thing? Brenda wondered. He is so absolutely cute with his pug-shaped face, almost human lips and floppy ears. He seems gentle enough, she observed, checking to see if the dog had a collar or any tags. There were none. Totally perplexed, Brenda decided that there was nothing she could do until morning. So, she got back in bed squeezing her feet to the left of the dog, who had obviously staked out his resting place for the remainder of the night. In a few minutes, Brenda drifted off to the most peaceful and happiest sleep she ever had.

The next morning, Brenda awoke to the sound of snoring. For a moment, she was puzzled. Then, she looked toward the bottom of her air mattress and saw the dog laying on its side with all four legs stretched out snoring and snorting in its sleep. She laughed at the sight and sounds and gave the pup a gentle nudge under the covers with her feet. The dog rolled over, giving Brenda a look of annoyance. It got down on the tent floor, stretched, yawned and walked up opposite Brenda's head where it sat and gave her a penetrating look.

His eyes, Brenda thought. They are almost human and seem to be looking right into my soul. It is as though he is trying to tell me something. Oh! Maybe he has to pee, she thought. I don't want him going in the tent. She got up noticing that the rain had stopped. She slipped into a pair of shorts and began unzipping the front flap when it dawned on her that there was no way to restrain the dog once it left the tent. However, when the dog began sniffing around inside, she realized that if she did not want to clean up after it, she had no choice except to take it outside.

As soon as Brenda opened the flap, the dog ran out and began sniffing around the other tents and shelters. Traffic was already whizzing by on Main Street. She was terrified that the dog would dart out into the traffic and be hurt. However, the dog scurried between two adjacent tents into the grass of the park where it first found a light pole to its liking and then circled around in the grass a couple of times adopting a familiar position. Much to Brenda's relief, when the dog had finished its business, it made a dart back to her and without any prompting jumped back into her tent.

By this time, some of the other Hanford Heights residents were waking up. Brenda could hear them shuffling and moving about as they began their daily routine. The smell of coffee was in the air letting her know that a couple of shelters away Little Willie was up brewing a cup or two on his propane camp stove. Brenda was not a coffee person. She preferred to drink plain, bottled water or caffeine-free cola. But, she was also hungry. She took a plastic bowl from her makeshift cabinet and filled it halfway with cornflakes. Then she took a large tablespoon of instant powdered milk and spread it over the cereal. Next, she added a half cup of water, stirred it and presto, she had cereal with milk. Lastly, she topped the cereal with a few blueberries and began to enjoy her breakfast. That is until she noticed the mournful look the dog was giving her.

"Oh my, what am I going to give you for breakfast?" Brenda wondered aloud. She felt awkward eating the cereal while the poor dog just sat there and stared at her. She had read somewhere that most dogs are glucose intolerant, so they should not be given milk. Then it dawned on her, most dogs love peanut butter. Quickly finishing her cereal, Brenda took a couple of soda crackers from the cabinet, opened the peanut butter jar and spread peanut butter on one of the crackers. She broke off a piece and offered it to the dog, who stood up and wagged its tail as it obviously relished the treat. However, after devouring both peanut butter crackers, the dog was making funny motions trying to cope with the peanut butter sticking to the roof of its mouth. Brenda rinsed out her cereal bowl, filled it with water and pushed the bowl toward the dog, who promptly lapped up almost all of the water. Then, the dog hopped back up on Brenda's bedding and contentedly curled itself in a resting position.

"Hey Honey! You gonna stay in there all day or are ya gonna come on out and visit wit the rest of us?" Mamma Louise hollered as she approached Brenda's tent.

The response from Brenda's tent was a series of loud, sharp barks that frightened the stuffing out of Mamma Louise.

"What the hell you got in there?" Mamma Louise shouted. "A wolf hound? " Then in a voice filled with concern, she added, "You OK baby?"

By this time, several of Brenda's other neighbors had joined Mamma Louise at the front of her tent. The barking from inside the tent continued sporadically as Brenda slowly unzipped the front flap. As the flap was pulled aside, Brenda stuck her smiling face out and said, "I'm just fine, thank you." A moment later, a small furry, brown and white pug face with big brown eyes nuzzled its way next to Brenda and gave one last round of barks to announce its arrival.

"Well, can you beat that? A dog!" Rosario exclaimed.

Horace, who could be a real grump but who would give his last possession to help someone in need, growled, "Can't you keep that thing quiet? It's making enough noise to wake the dead!"

Alicia, who was the first homeless person to befriend Brenda, stepped up nose to nose with Horace and said, "That's not a 'thing.' It's a puppy dog and a damn cute one at that."

Old Billy Joe steadied himself on his crutch. He was a Viet Nam veteran, or so he said, and claimed an

17

enemy bullet smashed his right kneecap so bad he could not walk without the help of a crutch. Not everyone believed his story, though. It was rumored what really happened was that he never served in the Army at all. Rather, he ran off to Canada to avoid the draft and busted his leg pretty bad in a motorcycle accident.

"Where did you get that fine dog, Brenda? Does it have a name?" Billy Joe asked.

"Billy Joe, I swear it just came to my tent last night to get out of the rain. I have no idea where it came from or what to do about it. And, if it has a name, I don't know what it is."

The dog was now fully outside the tent. It seemed fascinated by all of the attention and gave no indication that it would run away. Rosario and Angelina came over and petted the animal, who seemed to enjoy every minute of it.

"He must belong to somebody," Brenda opined. "Don't you think we should try to find the owner?" she said in a voice that lacked conviction.

"Well, the next time the cops come by we could mention it to them. But, how do we know one of them wouldn't just take the little guy for her own?"

"We could keep him here," Horace said, surprising the others. "I mean between all of us there would be plenty of food for him."

"Oh my, Horace. You do have a heart, after all," Rosario said. The others laughed while Horace grumbled at Rosario's snide comment.

"He really should be Brenda's dog," Horace said. "She was the one who found him."

Brenda's heart quickened at the thought of having a dog. "I really did not find him," she explained. "He just wanted to get out of the rain. He could have gone to any of your places."

Mamma Louise had a suggestion. "Maybe in a way we could all take turns caring for him with the understanding that he is really Brenda's dog," she said.

"I like that idea," Billy Joe said.

"Me too," Alicia added. "We can all help take care of him but he can live in Brenda's tent – if she that's what she wants."

Brenda was quick to say that was a great idea and that anytime anybody wanted him to stay with them for a while, that would be fine, too.

"Hey, what do you guys have there?" asked Little Willie, who was munching on a chocolate cream wafer he just pulled out of an Oreo bag as he strolled over.

"It's a dog, Willie. You can see that. A little male. Brenda took him in during the storm last night."

"He was scratching at my tent trying to get out of the rain, Willie. He must be a stray. We were just talking what to do with him. What do you think?"

"I'd keep him," Little Willie said. He got his moniker because of his size. At 4' 11," he was the shortest person in the group – male or female. "But, there are a couple of things. We can't just call him 'dog.' He has to have a name. Also, we can't let him run around loose. He

19

could run out into traffic and get killed or you can bet the animal control people would chase him down and take him to the Humane Society Shelter."

"That's right, Willie," Alicia agreed. "Or, he might run away and get lost. Anyway, we'd lose him. So, we need to get him a leash and a collar."

"Do you want a treat, little guy?" Little Willie asked the dog, as he offered the animal half an Oreo. The dog wolfed the cookie down in one gulp and before Little Willie could react, stuck its face into the Oreo bag trying to get another treat.

"That would be a good name for him, Willie," Angeline said. "He's brown and white just like the cookie. Why don't we call him Oreo?"

"Well, be careful there," Alicia cautioned. "Oreo has another meaning, as well, and that one is not as nice as the cookie."

"Bah," Horace said. "That kind of Oreo is human. This one is a dog and I think it fits him perfectly."

Brenda was beside herself with joy. She bent over, picked up the dog and raised him over her head. "Look everybody, we have our very own puppy dog." Lowering the dog so she could hug him, she said, "Welcome to Hanford Heights, Oreo!" Every one applauded and chimed in, "Welcome, Oreo!"

Oreo squirmed out of Brenda's arms and jumped to the ground. He made a beeline for the light pole he had found earlier that morning. After nearly losing his balance standing on three legs, he ran back to the group, sat down wagged his tail in delight and begged for another cookie.

"Not too many treats," Old Billie Joe warned. "We don't want him to get worms."

And then, something remarkable happened. More of the homeless in the Heights began coming over to the area of the park where the others had gathered. They asked what was happening and were told about the dog and how it suddenly showed up during the rain; how Brenda took it in; and, now how it was decided that although Brenda had first rights to the animal, it was sort of everyone's dog. Everyone in the camp thought that Oreo was a great name for the little creature. A rather unkempt woman went back to her shelter and returned with a collar and leash that had once belonged to her long gone pet. It was a gift for Oreo, she said.

Another person, contributed a can of salmon. "Salmon is really good for dogs," she said. "Lots of Omega-3 fats. That's good for his heart and a nice shiny coat."

Still another Heights resident fetched a large flat pillow from her shelter and gave it to Brenda. "This will make a nice bed for him," she said.

And, so it went. Several asked if they could take Oreo for a walk. One contributed a bowl for his water. Another gave Brenda a brush for his hair. Some said they would be happy to take care of Oreo when Brenda had to go for her appointment at the Hanford Metro Women's Shelter. But, what was most amazing was that almost everyone suddenly had someone else, albeit a little dog, that was more helpless and vulnerable than themselves that needed their love and help. And, this was just the beginning.

Saint Oreo

Chapter Three

Hanford Heights residents were always moving in and out of the homeless camp. The current population of the Heights was now down to nineteen. Although that was not a large number, the combination of tents and makeshift shelters stretched for well over 200 feet on the east side of Hanford Park along Main Street. Much to the dismay of the City Council, the homeless camp attracted sightseers who drove by day and night, tying up traffic as they stopped to take photographs of the pathetic scene. Their filming interest focused mostly on the accumulation of trash, refuse, empty whisky bottles, human waste and occasional hypodermic needles from the few in the camp who used hard drugs. But, over the past few days, things in the camp slowly began to change.

The first and most noticeable change was that the residents cleaned up much of the disgusting accumulated matter that people had to carefully avoid as they walked pass the homeless shelters. People were puzzled by this because it was not the kind of behavior one would expect from trashy homeless people. The real reason was quite simple. The Heights homeless did not want their new camp mascot, a beautiful and playful little dog named Oreo, to get into something that would hurt him.

People who had a better view of the park, such as those who worked in the high-rise office buildings facing it, were also able to observe the strange sight of homeless people taking turns walking and playing with the dog. The little creature especially loved to play fetch when someone threw a tennis ball onto the park lawn. Even more remarkable, several homeless people were spotted picking up the little animal's litter and actually depositing it in a park trash barrel. None of this fit the stereotype image that many people had formed about how the homeless behave. It was not long before this phenomenon came to the attention of the news media.

One day a news van with a satellite dish on its top pulled up to the park. The satellite dish was raised and two people got out of the van, one a very attractive younger woman holding a microphone, and the other her driver and cameraman. The woman, who identified herself as Megan Kinlaw, positioned herself in front of the trashiest of the makeshift shelters. She began narrating something as her cameraman panned between her and the other tents and shelters. The cameraman seemed flustered when he could not find the expected human waste, used needles and other trash to capture for the TV audience.

Megan and the cameraman then moved between two tents to the open park lawn and began filming two homeless people, who turned out to be Brenda and Mamma Louise, taking turns throwing a tennis ball out onto the park lawn as a little brown and white dog did its best to chase it down. Several other of the Height's homeless stood back laughing and applauding each time the dog secured the ball in its mouth and returned it to either Brenda or Mamma Louise. The news team focused on that scene until the little dog obviously had enough exercise and laid down on the grass, refusing to chase any more balls – at least for the moment.

Brenda and Mamma Louise were joined by Billie Joe and Rosario, who was holding Oreo's leash. Megan Kinlaw and her cameraman rushed over to the group. She asked Mamma Louise a couple of insensitive questions and practically pushed her microphone in the latter's face to record her response. Meanwhile, the cameraman was getting a close-up of all the action.

"What you mean, what I think about the homeless camping in the park?" Mamma Louise responded, obviously annoyed. "Woman, look over there at that blue and white tent," she said pointing at a small two person camping tent. "That's where I live and I ain't homeless because that is my home!" she said laughing.

"I guess by your standards we are all homeless," Rosario added. "Truth is, we all got a place to live, of sorts, and we all be one big happy family." Billie Joe, Brenda and Mamma Louise all shook their heads in agreement and muttered "Oh yeah!" and "Amen."

This totally bewildered Megan Kinlaw and her cameraman who were recording the scene to be shown on Hanford Channel 7's evening news broadcast.

"But, I don't understand," Megan said. "This is not the scene I remember when I walked by here myself barely a month ago. Then, there was trash and worse all over the sidewalk. And, I do not remember any of you playing fetch with a dog."

"That's true," Angelina said as she, Horace and several other Heights residents came over to see what was going on.

"But that was before Oreo arrived."

"Who is Oreo?" Megan inquired.

Brenda pointed to the dog who was now contentedly lying still with the tennis ball in its mouth, as if meditating about something.

"Him? That little Shih Tzu?" Megan asked.

"What did you call Oreo?" Rosario asked.

"A Shih Tzu," Megan replied. "That's his breed. You can tell by the pug face, big brown eyes, floppy ears, fluffy tail and his beautiful coat of hair."

"You mean fur, don't you?" Rosario said.

"No. Shih Tzu is a breed of dogs that have actual hair – not fur. Because of that they do not shed," Megan explained as she walked over to Oreo accompanied by her cameraman, who zoomed in on the animal. "He is absolutely adorable," she said. "But, what does he have to do with any of this."

Oreo suddenly stood up, fully alert as though expecting something.

Rosario continued, "I guess you would have had to live here at the Heights in order to understand…" She was cut off by a screeching of brakes on Main Street on the west side of the park accompanied by a woman's scream and cry of anguish. Oreo dropped the tennis ball he held in his mouth and ran as fast as his little legs could carry him toward the sound of the incident. Brenda, Billie Joe, Mamma Louise and Rosario scurried after him, Brenda calling unsuccessfully for Oreo to "Stay." Not surprisingly, Megan and her cameraman followed as fast as they could, as well.

They all arrived to witness a tragic scene. A little dachshund had broken loose from its owner, ran out into the street and was hit by a car. The dog's owner was in tears as she looked at the inert body of her beloved pet.

"I'm so sorry!" the man driving the car that struck the dog said. "She ran out in front of me before I could stop."

The woman who owned the dachshund nodded in understanding but was crying uncontrollably. A bystander picked the dog up from the street and placed it on the grass under a park tree. Megan's cameraman was filming the entire unfolding scene.

Then, unexpectedly, Oreo walked over to the dog and began sniffing it. He licked the dog's face repeatedly, stood back, barked and wagged his tail. Someone in the crowd that had gathered shouted, "It's moving! It's not dead!"

There was a collective gasp from the crowd as the dachshund shuddered a little then blinked its eyes and began slowly moving its head and paws. The woman who owned the dog ran over to it, picked it up and said over and over, "Molly I love you!" She was crying, but this time the tears were of joy.

Oreo barked again, his tail wagging as though he had just been given his most favored treat. Then, someone else shouted, "That little brown and white dog must have revived it when he licked its face."

"Not a chance," said the bystander who had carried the dachshund from the street and placed it under the tree. I guarantee you that dog was dead. It was not breathing and it had blood in its nose and mouth. I don't see any blood there now."

Brenda knelt down on the ground and called Oreo over to her. She scratched his ears and petted his head. "Oreo, you little angel, did you do this?" she asked in wonder. Oreo simply looked at Brenda with his big brown eyes and continued to wag his fluffy tail.

Manny Ortega, another homeless resident of the Heights, crossed himself and said, "*Esto es un milagro!* It is a miracle!"

Megan Kinlaw motioned for her cameraman to focus on her. She looked directly at the camera speaking into her microphone, "Ladies and gentlemen, I don't know what is happening here but we have just witnessed something extraordinary. Just a few minutes ago, one of the residents of the Heights in Hanford Park attributed the positive change that seems to have come over the homeless here to the little Shih Tzu named Oreo you can see here," the cameraman switched momentarily to the dog then pointed the camera again at Megan.

"Now, we have this unexplainable situation where to all outward appearances Oreo did something to revive that little dachshund the woman you see over there is holding that had been hit by a car and seemed to be dead. I don't know what to say." Then, Megan signaled to cameraman to stop filming as she succumbed to the emotion of the moment and began sniffling, herself.

On Hanford Channel 7's evening news that night, the story about the homeless people who were camping out at Hanford Park and a little dog named Oreo were the featured story. It was a story that touched the hearts of many of Channel 7's viewers. However, it also left many unanswered questions. Who was this little dog called Oreo? Where did it come from? Did it possess any special powers? TV viewers watching the news that night shook their heads in amazement, but then went on with their usual evening routines. However, the story was picked up by national news and later that night, the major networks all ran a short clip about the remarkable event that day at the park in the city of Hanford.

Even more remarkable, later that night two or three dozen people of all ages gathered in the park at the tree under which Molly, the dachshund had been laid after being hit. All carried candles and a few placed flowers at the spot. They also placed makeshift signs that read:

Oreo we love you

God bless Oreo and Molly

Oreo, you are an angel

A miracle happened today

Some of the people who gathered in the park walked over to the homeless camp and called out Oreo's name. However, Oreo was securely in Brenda's tent and she neither responded nor allowed him to go out. Finally, Horace and Little Willie shooed the people away; but, not before one of the crowd said, "You had better keep an eye on that miracle-working pup. Someone else is going to want it for themselves." Horace gruffly shouted, "You best be getting out of here now!" However, Brenda overheard what the man said and shuddered at the thought. She picked up Oreo and held him close to her breast.

Saint Oreo

Chapter Four

After a few days, the news media began to lose interest in Oreo, the incident with Molly the dachshund and the plight of the homeless at Hanford Heights. But, that was not the end of it, by far. In fact, much to the annoyance of the Hanford City Council and a number of local religious organizations, the word spread that there was a little brown and white dog named Oreo living among the homeless camped in Hanford Park that had the miraculous power to heal other animals. In addition, it was noted, the little dog seemed to have an unexplainable, positive affect on the homeless population there.

The result was a growing stream of people bringing their sick or injured pets to the Heights looking for Oreo. They left small gifts such as dog food, treats, a new collar and leash and even knitted puppy sweaters at the tree where the supposed miracle occurred. Whenever, one of the pets they brought recovered, they would claim that Oreo had something to do with it. If the pet did not recover, well that must just be fate. It certainly was not Oreo's fault. Then, one day a little after noon, a food truck marked *Benny's Lunches* pulled up in front of the cluster of tents and shelters and sounded its melodious horn.

Alicia was the first to leave her shelter to see what all the ruckus was about. "What you do'n here?" she asked the food truck driver. "This ain't no place for a food truck!"

Benny jumped down from the cab of the truck. He went around to the back and lifted the sliding rear panel of the truck. Then he climbed inside and threw open the two side panels. "Sweetheart, you better get used to it. Mrs. Van Gulden is paying me to drive this truck here for the rest of the summer and to give all of you whatever you want from the menu you see right there," he said, pointing to the large menu on the outside of the truck featuring sandwiches, subs, gyros, fries and much more.

"We ain't got no money for that, as good as it looks," Billie Joe chimed in. "And, who is this Mrs. Van Gulden, anyway?"

"Mrs. Van Gulden?" Benny repeated. "She lives over there in one of those big Victorian houses on the other side of the park. She is convinced your mutt saved her dog Molly's life and she's mighty grateful."

"Damn, that's mighty nice of that woman," Little Willie said. "No sense looking a gift horse in the mouth. I'll have me one of them Italian Subs, please."

"Sure thing," Benny replied, as Mamma Louise walked up leading Oreo on his new leash. "A ham Gyro for me, kindly," she said. Then she added, "With an order of fries and a diet cola."

"How about something for the little guy?" Manny Ortega asked, referring to Oreo.

"Oh, don't worry about him!" Benny exclaimed. "Mrs. Gulden told me he gets boiled chicken with rice, sliced roasted turkey breast or sliced top round. I'm supposed to rotate this fine selection every day." Benny reached under the counter he was working at and retrieved a patterned porcelain dog dish with the name Oreo hand painted on it. "He even has his own dish!" Benny added.

By now, most of the homeless camp had gathered around the food truck and lined up to get their one full, wholesome meal for the day. They insisted that Oreo be put in the front of the line since it was because of him they were receiving this windfall. Mamma Louise hollered for Brenda to come forward and the two marched up to the front of the line, led by an obviously hungry Shih Tzu that was already licking its lips with a tongue long enough to reach to the tip of its nose. "Wait till Hanford Channel 7 hears about this one," Angelina said.

***

Hanford was not a large town. Its population was only about 45,000. The Hanford Municipal Building, built in 1873, was located at the very north part of Main Street. It was the first significant building people saw as they entered town from the north. The other structures at that end of town were a small strip mall, a gas station and a used car dealership. The three-story municipal building was of brick construction in the Romanesque Revival style. The entrance to the building was protected by a large stone arch that faced a thirty-five foot Civil War monument in the shape of a pillar. Immediately inside the arch, visitors, or anyone doing business in the building, climbed stairs to the right or left of the arch in order to reach the building's business areas. A handicapped elevator entrance could be accessed just past either set of stairs.

As seat of Travis County, the Municipal Building housed the county court house and a variety of municipal and county offices such as tax collector, supervisor of elections, public works, clerk of court and, of course, the Hanford City Council. Despite the age of the building, it was in remarkably good repair. Further, it had been renovated as recently as 2012.

Charlie Meacham, chairman of the eight member Council, slammed the gavel down on the desk in front of him bringing the specially called council meeting to order. Charlie was annoyed as hell and made no bones about it.

"Because of a damn dog," Charlie began, "We find it necessary to call this session to order so that we can discuss what is to be done with that filthy homeless camp squatting on public land on Hanford Park." Charlie was obviously disgusted with the entire matter – dog and homeless together.

"Mr. Chairman," Rachael Owens, Director of the Hanford Metro Women's Shelter and a Council member said, raising her hand to be recognized.

"Yes Rachael, what is it?" Charlie asked, further annoyed at being interrupted when he had just begun to speak.

"Charlie, you have to remember that those people are not camping on park grounds. Their tents and shelters, are on the sidewalk, which is accessible to anyone at any time of the day. Overnight camping is prohibited only on the park ground, itself."

"Yes, you are right, Rachael. We went head-to-head with the ACLU on that one. I stand corrected."

Zack Reynolds, another Council member, was recognized and said, "I agree that it seems this whole issue was caused by a dog the news media fell in love with. However, we really need to do something to clean up what they call Hanford Heights. The people of Hanford are really pissed about this. So, I have a couple of ideas I would like to present to the Council..."

And, so it went. The Council met for over an hour. They studied several alternative proposals before concluding that their action had to be in two phases. The first phase was to immediately take visible action to pacify the public outcry initiated by the news media's reporting about a little dog named Oreo that was having a major impact on the homeless in the Heights. That phase would be mostly cosmetic – but it was something needed.

The second phase would be a more permanent solution. However, it would require joint action by not only the City Council, but also local organizations like the Women's Shelter, Mission Church, Catholic Charities, Beacon Lighthouse and others. Satisfied that they had accomplished something useful, the Council adjourned. Unfortunately, the Council did not receive all of the credit they deserved. That night, the Hanford Times Reporter newspaper ran a featured article titled, *Miracle Dog Forces Council to Act*. When Charlie Meacham read the article before dinner, he crumbled the page it was on, threw it in the trash and poured himself a double bourbon. "Damn dog!" he said, tossing the drink down his throat in complete frustration. Then he refilled his glass and tried to read the rest of the paper.

The next day, a Mid-West Sanitation Service truck stopped in front of the homeless shelters along the park. Using a forklift, the driver unloaded a half dozen portable toilets, which he lined up neatly on the sidewalk at the end of the shelters. After finishing his task and without saying a word to the curious onlookers, he got back in his truck and drove off.

On the following day, another truck drove up to the homeless complex and unloaded twenty boxes, each marked with a familiar camping equipment logo and marked "4 Person Dome Tent with Easy Set Up Kit." Accompanying the truck was a car driven by an employee of the Hanford Parks and Recreation Department who got out and asked that all of the homeless assemble for a message from the department's director.

When the Height's residents assembled, the man said that the tents were being supplied to the homeless free of charge. They were not required to accept them; however, he pointed out that at least half of the makeshift shelters in the camp were unsanitary, leaked when it rained and provided little privacy and protection to their owners. The tents, he said, were spacious, comfortable, safe and secure. Fifteen of the nineteen Heights residents accepted the city's offer. Brenda, who already had a tent she considered sufficient and comfortable, was one of the few who declined the offer.

That night, Charlie Meacham appeared on Hanford Channel 7 with Megan Kinlaw. He told the viewing audience that the City Council has always been concerned about the welfare of the residents of Hanford, including the unfortunate homeless who had been camping at the Heights. He said that by the end of summer a permanent solution to the homeless problem would be announced. In the meantime, the portable toilets and tents and the generous gift of a daily food truck would help ensure the homeless had safe, sanitary and reasonably comfortable living conditions.

Megan Kinlaw asked if the attention that had been given to Oreo, now known as the homeless camp's champion, had anything to do with the Council's decision. Meacham turned red with controlled anger. Calmly, he said the Council had been planning to do something like this for a long time. Megan pressed Meacham further and asked if the Council believed there was something special about Oreo, something that could not be easily explained. Meacham scuffed at her suggestion and testily said, "If it looks like a dog, barks like a dog and acts like a dog then it damn well is a dog and nothing more!"

***

The food truck was due anytime now and most of the Height's residents were already lining up. Absent was Oreo, who had wandered off somewhere. No one worried about him because he always came back, especially at lunchtime. No one except Brenda, that is. She still recalled the warning she heard a few days ago that there were those who would like to get their hands on Oreo because they considered the "miracle" dog to be valuable enough to steal.

As the food truck rolled up, Oreo strolled toward the group trailed by a pathetic looking mixed-breed, tan colored, very pregnant female Retriever that looked like she was ready to deliver her litter momentarily. Oreo boldly marched to the front of the line with the female Retriever in tow. When Benny threw open the side panel of the truck signaling that chow was ready, Oreo sat down, looking back and forth between the truck and his guest. The message was clear. She needs food.

"I don't believe that dog," Manny Ortega said, shaking his head in amazement at Oreo. "I'll bet the bitch is homeless, too."

"Yeah, sure looks like it," Rosario said. "Bet her old man ran off on her when he found out he knocked her up!" she exclaimed.

"Just like yours did, Rosie," Alicia hollered. Everyone laughed.

"Shut up you dumb-assed slut!" Rosario retorted. "He didn't run off. He got 5-0'd and they put him in the slammer. Still there as best I know," she said explaining that he had been arrested and jailed. Everyone in the food line roared.

Oreo was whining with impatience now. He moved over and sat next to the female Retriever.

Benny filled Oreo's bowl and passed it to Manny who was first in line. "Let's see what happens when you give it to him, Manny," he said.

Manny dutifully carried the bowl over to Oreo who sat impassively looking at it, sniffing the contents. Then he moved a away a little and the Retriever hungrily went over and in a flash devoured everything in the bowl. "Wow! She must have been hungry!" Manny said.

Benny refilled Oreo's bowl and this time he ate his fill. Brenda brought over two bowls from her tent and filled them both with bottled water. Both dogs lapped up the water eagerly.

"What we gonna do wit that one, now?" Mamma Louise wondered aloud.

"She sure look like she gonna drop her pups any minute now," Angelina observed. "We better find a place for her."

They all finished their free lunches and then decided to make a place for the dog between Alicia's and Horace's tents. Horace found a cardboard box in a trash bin a block away and cut the top flaps and one side flap so the dog could come and go at will. A woman named Hanna, from further down the line of tents, contributed a big towel for the dog to lay on and Little Willie fashioned a tent-like cover for the box in case it rained.

"She doesn't have a collar or tag or anything," Billie Joe said. "We have to call her something."

"How about Daisy," Manny suggested.

"Daisy! Why Daisy?" Alicia asked.

"Damn if I know," Manny replied. "Just popped in my head."

They all agreed that Daisy was probably as good as any name. So, Alicia led Daisy to her new, but likely temporary, home and was pleased to see that the dog ambled after her quite willingly. Oreo followed as though supervising the whole matter.

At daybreak the next morning, Alicia was awaken by the sound of whining coming from Daisy's box. She got up, went outside and raised the cover Little Willie made and shouted loud enough to wake the whole camp, "Daisy has puppies!" Within minutes, everyone ran out of their tents, some half-clothed, and rushed over to Daisy's box. Inside was a very proud tan Retriever nursing six beautiful tan puppies. The women cried, the men gaped at the scene and then they all applauded. Oreo sat off to the side, out of the limelight that was reserved for the dog he led to a place where he knew she would get help.

***

They came just after midnight. There were three of them. They went from tent to tent demanding "the dog." They ripped open tent entrance flaps, shinning flashlights at the terrified occupants looking for "the dog." Brenda woke with a start and made sure Oreo was with her.

When the intruders found Daisy's box one of them said, "There it is!" But, another said, "No idiot. The one we want is brown and white."

Brenda was terrified. She knew they were coming for Oreo. There was no way, though, she was going to let them take him away. She grabbed Oreo and hugged him tightly. "You are an angel, Oreo. I know God will protect you." Oreo looked at her with his beautiful, knowing eyes and wagged his tail.

Brenda heard Angelina swear at the intruders as they moved down the line of tents.

"Stay put, old man, or I'll blow your head off," one of them said to Horace when he began to rise from his sleeping bag.

Brenda quietly unzipped the front flap of her tent and let Oreo out. "Run Oreo! Run!" she shouted. Oreo turned toward Brenda, barked and wagged his fluffy tail and then ran off into the safety of the darkness.

Chapter Five

His Most Reverend Excellency John O'Connor, Bishop of the Diocese of Brookfield, Illinois, put down the newspaper he had been reading and took another drink of coffee from his favorite mug. An hour earlier, he had finished breakfast after celebrating the 7:30 am Holy Mass at St. Barnard's Cathedral in Brookfield. Now, he was enjoying his second cup of coffee for the day in the company of his assistant, Monsignor Carl Obermann. Obermann, age 43, was one of the youngest monsignors in the diocese. Luckily for him, he was given the honorific Monsignor by Pope Benedict XVI shortly before that pope stepped down and a new pontiff, Pope Francis, was elected by the College of Cardinals. One of Pope Francis' first acts was to restrict the granting of the honorific to priests over the age of sixty-five, thus nearly abolishing what previously had been a common practice.

"What do you think about that mess in Hanford, Carl?" the bishop asked his assistant.

"You mean the theft from the poor boxes at St. Albans?" Obermann inquired.

"No, the police will take care of that," the bishop responded. "I mean about the fuss being made over that dog – the one they call Oreo."

"Ah, that one," Obermann said as he took another bite out of a chocolate filled croissant that had been on a plate on the coffee table in front of him. "Well, as I understand it, it is a non-matter. The dog seems to have disappeared. No one has seen it for a few days, now."

"The news media is still talking about it," the bishop said. "They are making the dog to be something almost mystical."

"Unfortunately, so are some Catholics," Obermann observed. "People are still visiting Hanford Park and leaving offerings or lighting vigil candles – to the dog, mind you."

"We don't really know if those people are Catholics, though," the bishop countered.

"I can tell you this, Your Excellency, just yesterday Father Watkins at Our Lady of the Grove parish in Hanford told me that a couple of his parishioners wanted a Mass to be offered for the intention of a dog named Oreo – that he be protected from harm."

"The Church does not allow a Mass to be offered for the intention of a non-human," the bishop stated emphatically.

"Yes, of course," Obermann said. "You know, if we are not careful this whole thing about the dog could wind up in some kind of a cult," he speculated. "Don't forget, in certain countries and cultures animals are considered sacred. In India, for example, cows are revered by Hindus and the Thais revere white elephants. It was much more so in ancient cultures like when the Aztecs worshipped the jaguar and the Celts in Western Europe worshiped the wild boar."

The bishop laughed. "Calm down Carl. This is just a dog. Still, I find it all somewhat unsettling. Look, why don't you take a ride down to Hanford and take George Watkins out to dinner. Invite, Charlie Bennett at St. Andrew's, too. Then let's discuss what you find out about this creature called Oreo."

The bishop had the practice of referring to the priests in his diocese by their first names. When in private, such as when he and a select few of the older priests met at the bishop's residence for a monthly game of five-card stud poker, they called him by his first name, John or even Johnnie for those priests he grew up with. However, to all of the other priests, he was referred to more formally by the customary title Your Excellency.

A few days later, the bishop and monsignor were once again relaxing in the bishop's study. Monsignor Obermann picked through the cocktail nuts in the dish on the coffee table, selecting only the cashews. A confirmed coffee drinker, he had just poured himself his third of four customary daily cups of the rich, stimulating beverage. For his part, the bishop was nursing a scotch on the rocks.

"So, there might be something to the story, then," the bishop said.

"Actually, much of it can be explained to coincidence. However, there could be a psychological aspect to it as well."

"You are referring to the effect the dog had on that particular homeless population?" the bishop suggested.

"Yes. There have been studies that show a correlation between a positive life event and improvement in psychological disorder. In essence, a positive life event can serve as a stress buffer by generating positive feelings," Obermann explained.

" I see," the bishop said pensively. "The positive event might have been that for the first time those homeless people discovered they were actually needed: the lost, helpless dog needed their love and care."

"Exactly. As a result, they put aside their own problems and dysfunctions in order to ensure the safety and well-being of the dog."

"Remarkable!" The bishop said. "However, you have to wonder how it was that the dog Oreo appeared at that particular place and that particular time. At the very least, according to the psychological theory you just presented, he was the catalyst for the positive behavioral change among the homeless group."

Overmann nodded in agreement. "Not just that group," he said. "There was a domino effect that spilled over to the whole community, their attitude toward the homeless and even to actions taken by the Hanford City Council."

"By the way, what has happened to the young woman Brenda Hopkins who either found the dog or was found by it?"

"The homeless group unanimously agreed she should have one of the Retriever puppies to help her compensate for the loss of Oreo. She then went to the Hanford Metro Women's Shelter and told them she would like to take advantage of their offer to move there if they would allow her to keep the puppy. She told them she wanted to take coding classes to develop new skills and get on with her life. They welcomed her and the puppy."

"Marvelous!" the bishop exclaimed. "And the other homeless?"

"A couple of the women followed Brenda to the Women's Shelter and one or two of the men took jobs offered them through the auspices of the Mission Church," Obermann answered. "The local charities are still trying to work with the rest of them."

The bishop nodded. "But, that still leaves the incident with the dachshund – the one called Molly."

"Yes," Obermann agreed. "And that is, perhaps, the most perplexing of all that happened."

"Animals can be more resilient that some of us might imagine," the bishop said.

"But, not this one," Obermann replied, looking the bishop straight in the eyes. "I personally spoke to the man who picked up the dachshund's body and moved it to the park lawn under the tree. He is an Emergency Medical Technician and works for the Hanford Fire Department. The man has seen enough death to know if something is dead or alive. He swore to me that the dachshund was dead. No questions about it, he said."

The bishop sat back in his chair and took a long sip of his scotch. Thoughtfully, he said, "But, the Shih Tzu, the one they named Oreo, did nothing extraordinary."

"No," Obermann agreed. "He just went over to the body, sniffed it and licked the dead dog's face."

"Which is typical canine behavior," the bishop added. "Animals often instinctively lick the face of an injured companion in an attempt to revive it."

Obermann just looked at the bishop saying nothing.

"Did you speak with the owner of the dachshund?" the bishop asked.

"Yes. She said all the while Oreo was seemingly attending to her dog Molly, she was praying to St. Francis to intercede with the Lord to save her dog."

"St. Francis," the bishop said as he looked intently at the monsignor. "Of course. St. Francis of Assisi, who among his other attributes, is the patron saint of the environment and animals because of his love of nature."

The bishop sighed. "Thank you, Carl. Good work. I really do not think there is anything to this that cannot be rationally explained. However, I believe the archbishop should be advised about the matter just for information purposes."

"Would you like me to summarize this in a short report to you?" Obermann asked.

"Yes, please do that. In some ways I would have liked to see this Oreo, myself. However, he seems to have disappeared and has not reappeared anywhere. So, this is obviously the end of it."

The bishop, however, was quite mistaken.

Chapter Six

The township of Cranston, Kansas, population 62,000, is located 255 miles west of Brookfield, not far where the rolling Missouri hills begin to give way to the Kansas plains. Cranston Children's Hospital sits at the western part of Cranston, offering patients, their families and visitors a remarkable view of the Coyote River, on which the hospital was located, as it flowed toward the southeast – especially at sunset.

A 290 bed facility, the hospital had a staff of 800 physicians and support personnel. It offered thirty-five pediatric subspecialties including neonatology, cardiology, pulmonology, infectious diseases, hematology, oncology, hospice and palliative medicine. Eight-year old Toby Ernst was a patient in Cranston Children's Hospital. He was suffering from acute lymphoblastic leukemia, a cancer that can be fatal if not treated promptly after diagnosis.

The problem was that Toby's leukemia was not diagnosed until after it had taken hold of his frail body. Doctors warned his parents, Bonnie and Edward Ernst, that the outlook for Toby was uncertain. There had been remission for a few short months, but it lapsed. Consequently, Dr. Elizabeth Gallo, a Board certified specialist in the disease, had ordered a lumbar puncture to learn if any cancer cells had worked their way into his spinal fluid. While Toby rested comfortably in Room 112 opposite the fourth floor nurses station, Dr. Gallo was meeting with Bonnie and Edward to give them the results of the test.

"I just checked on Toby, myself, a half-hour ago," Dr. Gallo said. "He is sleeping comfortably now. However, I am afraid that I do not have encouraging news."

Bonnie and Edward looked at each other apprehensively. "Does that mean you have bad news about the test?" Bonnie asked, holding back tears.

"Yes," Dr. Gallo replied solemnly. The two parents held each other's hand tightly. "There are leukemia cells in Toby's CSF, that is his Cerebral Spinal Fluid. That means that the leukemia has spread to the fluid that flows around his brain and spine." She waited for the stunned parents to react.

"Is that fatal?" Edward asked hesitantly.

"It can be," Dr. Gallo candidly replied. "However, there are new treatments that are available that our team is planning for Toby. Our next step is to begin a regime of radiation treatments designed to kill the leukemia cells that have spread to his spinal fluid. We will see how that works and go on from that point."

Bonnie was crying as Edward, who was trying to hold back his own tears, comforted her in his arms.

Over the next several days, Toby's prognosis was tentative. He had suffered much during the chemotherapy phase of his treatment. He had lost ten pounds, all of his hair and several of his teeth. Fortunately, those were his baby teeth, so the end result of that loss was he became several dollars richer thanks to the tooth fairy. However, he had become very depressed and began asking his mother what it was like to die. That tore at Bonnie's heart – certainly at Edward's, too – as they struggled further to confront the possibility he might not survive the cancer. With the help of a pediatric psychologist, Bonnie told Toby that death was just like going to sleep except that when you woke up all your pain would be gone and you would be in heaven with God and the angels. Toby thought that was pretty cool but said he hoped his mom and dad would be there with him. Edward assured him they would be. Then he and Bonnie went out of Toby's room into the hall and cried inconsolably.

One afternoon, Barbara Whitcomb, the pediatric psychologist on Dr. Gallo's team, suggested that Bonnie and Edward take Toby down to the hospital's large courtyard where a therapy dog park was located along the river front. She told them that every day at 3:00 pm, the animal handlers bring their pets together in the fenced dog park and allow them to run free and play. There was even a small, shallow pond where the dogs could jump in and romp to their hearts' content. Barbara Whitcomb thought that the sight of the dogs playing and having fun might boosts Toby's spirits. Something had to be done. It seemed that with each passing day, Toby was becoming more detached and withdrawn.

Bonnie and Edward readily agreed with Ms. Whitcomb's suggestion. They put Toby in a wheel chair and took him down to the first floor of the hospital's west wing. From there, they wound their way outside to the dog park. At first Toby was apathetic to his surroundings, as he had been so often before when his parents or a floor nurse took him outside for a breath of fresh air. However,

49

his eyes lit up when he saw the dogs playing. He asked his mother if she would push his wheelchair closer to the fence so he could get a better look at the dogs as they chased balls and Frisbees and each other. Suddenly, a green tennis ball came rolling across the grass toward Toby and stopped just inside the fence. A moment later it was pounced on by a lively brown and white dog that had floppy ears, large penetrating eyes, a pug nose and almost human lips. The dog picked up the ball in its mouth, turned and began to run back to join the other therapy dogs. But then, it stopped. It dropped the ball and came back to the fence opposite Toby.

The dog looked at Toby as though it was evaluating him. It sat down and cocked its head to one side, then to the other. Next, it stood up, its little fluffy tail wagging vigorously from one side to the other and barked. By now, it was clear that the dog had Toby's attention. He sat up the best he could and stretched his right arm and hand toward the animal pushing his fingers through the links of the fence. The dog, in turn, positioned itself immediately on the other side of the fence, front paws stretched out in front and rear end arched upward in the classic canine "let's play" mode. Bonnie swung the wheel chair around so the right wheel was touching the fence. Toby continued to stick the fingers of his right hand through a link in the fence, trying to touch the dog. As if accommodating Toby, the dog stood up again, moved closer to the fence, and gently licked Toby's fingers.

Toby clapped his hands in glee. Bonnie wiped tears of joy from her eyes with a tissue and hugged Edward, who was amazed at what he had just witnessed. It was the first time in so long that Toby had shown interest in anything, much less having exhibited any sign of pleasure. Then, one of the therapy dog handlers blew a whistle and all of the dogs bounded over to him to receive their afternoon treats. A big smile on his face, Toby looked up at his parents and asked, "Can we come here again tomorrow?" The joy and relief on the face of Toby's parents was unmistakable. "Yes, honey," Bonnie said. "We sure can."

The radiation treatment for Toby focused on the spinal column where leukemia cells had been detected. Sadly, Toby's body did not respond well to the treatment. He became excessively fatigued and had considerable nausea and headaches. He was also too ill to go outside to the dog park. Because of all of this, Dr. Gallo decided to stop those treatments after only two weeks. Soon after, however, Toby began perk up. He was doing much better eating solid food and actually gained a pound or two over the next several days. Most of all, he wanted to return to the dog park to see the little brown and white dog he had befriended – or who had befriended him.

Sure enough, whenever Toby was able to visit the dog park, the little dog would spot him and run over to the fence where he was. They seemed to play a private game together. The dog would bring a tennis ball over to the fence and drop it down close to where Toby was sitting on the other side. Then, the dog would back up a foot or two, sit down and give Toby a challenging look. Whenever Toby made a gesture like he was going to get the ball (actually there was no way he could reach it through the fence) the dog would rush over pick it up in its mouth and start the sequence all over again. Toby delighted in the game and beamed whenever the dog brought the ball close to him. Of course, there were also tender moments when Toby would put his fingers through a link in the fence and the little dog would lick his fingers.

As the days passed, Toby seemed to be improving. One day, Dr. Gallo told Bonnie and Edward that she had ordered a new set of tests to see whether the cancer had spread further. She took bone marrow samples, another blood test series and another lumber puncture. That was a lot of discomfort for a frail eight-year old boy who was so sick. The next day, when Bonnie and Edward were visiting Toby, Dr. Gallo said it was important that she go over the test results with them. They were stricken with apprehension as they sat in the doctor's office waiting for her report. When Dr. Gallo came into the room, Bonnie and Edward noted a perplexed look on her face and then the doctor broke out into a big smile.

"Mr. and Mrs. Ernst, I don't know what to say except that something remarkable has happened. The tests show that Toby is in complete remission. There is no trace of cancer cells anywhere!"

"Oh my God!" Bonnie said. "Are you sure?"

"As sure as I can be at this point," Dr. Gallo responded. "Toby's bone marrow now has only 4% blast cells, the blood tests are within normal range and we could not find any cancer cells in his spinal fluid." She put the papers with the test results on her desk and said, "Frankly, I have no idea how this is possible. Remissions most certainly do occur in cases like Toby's, but not this dramatically, especially considering that only a few weeks ago we were considering recommending that he be placed in our hospice and given only palliative care."

Bonnie and Edward did not care how Toby's complete remission came about. Nor were they interested in the technical details. They were filled with joy and gratitude and wanted to see their son. Dr. Gallo escorted them down the hall to Toby's room. As they approached his room, the nurses seated in the station across from it stood and applauded. Then, Bonnie and Edward noticed that a glittering banner with the words "Congratulations Toby!" was hung over the door to his room and inside were three other nurses, one with a cake she presented to the boy as his parents and the doctor walked into the room. But, as far as Bonnie and Edward were concerned, the best sight of all was seeing Toby sitting up on the lounge chair in his room, smiling with his arms outstretched to hug his parents. It was an absolutely wondrous moment!

***

Janan Taylor, Cranston Children's Hospital Community Relations Director, had just received a call from her husband, Mark, who was a pediatric oncology nurse. "I think you should come up here to Room 112 ASAP," Mark said. "I'll explain when you get here." Janan quickly summoned the hospital photographer Harry Smythe. "Harry," she said, "I think we may have a hot story for the Cranston Inquirer." With Harry and his camera in tow, Janan left her office and headed upstairs to the oncology floor.

In a ward where the atmosphere is somber more often than not, pediatric oncology was uncharacteristically festive when Janan and Harry arrived. Janan saw the banner over Room 112 and noticed several nurses standing outside the room smiling and chatting. "Hey Mark, what's going on?" Janan asked her husband. "Toby Ernst is in full remission." Mark said, pointing to the inside of the room, which was now a little crowded. "He'll be going home tomorrow. Just a month ago they were thinking about putting him hospice. But, it seems he has had a remarkable and unexpected recovery."

Janan walked into the room just as Toby, who was sitting up basking in all of the attention, asked his mother, "Mommy, when I get home can I have a puppy like Oreo?"

Janan felt a faint flicker of recognition at the name. "Who is Oreo, Toby," she asked.

Toby apparently did not hear the question. However, his father turned toward Janan and said, "Dr. Gallo felt it might help pull Toby out of the state of depression he was in if he could at least watch the dogs run loose and play in the park. So every day we took Toby down to the park where he could see them. Oreo is a little brown and white therapy dog in the dog park that caught Toby's interest."

Bonnie continued the explanation, "They seemed to strike up quite a friendship. Oreo usually came over to the fence where Toby was and in a way played with him. Toby was absolutely delighted! He loved every minute he was with the dog."

"I really think that helped Toby a lot," Bonnie said. "God bless that little dog." Then she turned back to Toby and said, "Yes, Toby. As soon as we get home we will get you a little puppy that looks just like Oreo."

"Harry, get some photos of Toby and all of this," Janan said, her arm sweeping the scene of celebration. "Then let's go down to the therapy dog office and talk with Myra. We need to get some photos of the dog Toby called Oreo." Before Janan and Harry left Toby's room, Janan asked Toby one more question. "Toby, how did you learn the dog's name was Oreo?"

"There is a thing around his neck," Toby said.

"He has a collar on with two tags hanging from it," Bonnie clarified. "One was a name tag in the shape of a bone and the other seemed to be a medal – I think it was a St. Francis medal."

Janan asked Bonnie and Edward a few more questions about the dog. Then, she wished them all of the best of happiness and began to leave the room.

"Oh, one more thing," Bonnie said. "If you have a chance to talk to the dog therapy people please tell them we are really impressed with the condition of all of those animals. They are so beautifully groomed."

Janan, nodded and left the room. On the way out, she gave Mark a kiss on the cheek and told him they were having homemade pasta for dinner. Mark gave her a thumb's up.

"You look troubled," Harry observed, as they were walking down the hallway.

"Yeah," Janan replied, her mind elsewhere. "I have heard the name Oreo before. I just can't place it."

"Cookies!" Harry laughed. "Haven't you ever eaten any of those delicious wafer cookies Nabisco makes.

Oreo is their brand name. I keep a bag of them in my office drawer!"

Janan joined him in laughing. "Yes, I know the brand. After we take some pictures of the dog we'll go back to your office and munch on a few," she said.

Myra Mitchell, who was in charge of the hospital's therapy dogs, was seated at her desk reviewing a couple of applications from dog owners who wanted to volunteer their pets for the program. She looked up when Janan and Harry walked into her office.

"Hi guys, what can I do for you?"

"Hi Myra," Janan replied. "We would like to get a few photos of Oreo if he is here today."

"Who or what is Oreo?" Myra asked.

"He is one of your therapy dogs," Janan said. "A little brown and white pup. According to Dr. Fowler, the relationship that developed between one of her leukemia patients, a little boy named Toby Ernst, and Oreo played a major role in the child's remarkable recovery. A month ago they were considering hospice for him. Now, he is in full remission."

"Janan, none of our dogs are named Oreo. What does he look like?"

"Umm, small breed about ten to fifteen pounds, floppy ears, penetrating brown eyes, a pug nose and face and a fluffy tail."

"Sounds like a Pomeranian, Cavalier or Shih Tzu," Myra said. "Probably the latter. But we do not have any of those here. We have fifteen therapy dogs and they are all out running loose in the park now. I know each of them and their owners or handlers. There is no Shih Tzu and no Oreo among them."

"I don't understand," Janan said, quite perplexed. "I spoke with Toby's parents and they said they frequently brought him down to the dog park. They told me Oreo would come over to the fence and sort of play with Toby. They were very certain about what the dog looked like. By the way," she added. "Mr. and Mrs. Ernst asked me to compliment you on the condition of the animals. Bonnie said they were impressed with their grooming, including Oreo's."

"That's nice to hear," Myra replied. "In fact, it is our policy to require all of the dogs to be bathed every week and most are groomed at least monthly."

Myra stood up, went to a cabinet and took out a file of photographs that she handed to Janan.

"I am glad the boy is in remission. However, I'm sorry. Your miracle dog Oreo is not registered in our therapy dog program. These are the only therapy dogs we have," she said as she handed Janan the photographs.

When Myra said "miracle dog," Janan's eyes lit up. "Oh my God," she exclaimed, recalling something she had seen on TV and in the press. Janan dropped the photographs on Myra's desk and rushed back to her office with Harry trailing behind.

Saint Oreo

Chapter Seven

Janan tore into her office and powered on her desktop computer. She waited impatiently for the lock screen to appear, cursing under her breath at the computer's slow boot speed. In less than a minute, a beautiful mountain meadow scene appeared accompanied by a logon prompt. Janan entered her password and as soon as the start page booted, she opened the Chrome browser and began searching for the name Oreo and the words "miracle dog." In a flash, she found what she was looking for – several articles and a TV news clip reporting on the unusual events that took place among homeless people and a little dog named Oreo at a Hanford, Illinois City Park a few weeks ago.

"I have the feeling that you have abandoned your thought about coming to my office and enjoying some of the Oreo cookies I have in my desk drawer, "Harry said. "Perhaps I had best be going."

Janan laughed. "Not yet. Wait just a minute." She was reading the articles as fast as she could. Then, she ran the five minute TV clip accompanying the articles. "There!" she said jubilantly. "There he is!"

"Who?" Harry asked as he peered over Janan's shoulders.

"Our miracle dog Oreo," Janan responded. "The camera shows him chasing a tennis ball that the tall man wearing a baseball cap just threw out onto the park lawn."

"I'll be damned." Harry said. "It sure looks like a little brown and white dog to me."

"Not just brown and white," Janan observed. "That is a Shih Tzu if I ever saw one."

"It can't possibly be the same dog that the Ernst family claim was playing with their son Toby, could it?" Harry asked. "Myra was emphatic that there was never a dog like that among her therapy dogs."

"I don't know," Janan said. "Can you pull out a few stills from that TV clip?"

"Sure," Harry said. "Better still, I can crop the photos and digitally enhance the images so that they will be clearer."

"Marvelous!" Janan said. "I owe you a family size bag of Oreo cookies. Let me know when you have finished. I want to take the photos to show Toby and his parents before they check out of the hospital tomorrow."

It only took Harry an hour to capture a half-dozen of the TV clip images and digitally enhance them. As soon as he printed glossy versions of them, he returned to Janan's office.

"Beautiful!" Janan said. "What an adorable little dog. Let's see if anyone in the Ernst family recognizes him."

A long walk back to pediatric oncology later, Janan and Harry stopped by Room 112, where Toby's parents were happily watching their eight-year old finish his dessert, a dish of lemon sherbet accompanied by a small piece of cake. They were amazed at how rapidly the boy's appetite was returning.

"Wow! If he keeps eating at that rate, he will put back on all those pounds he lost in just a few weeks," Janan said.

Bonnie and Edward smiled and nodded in agreement.

"Sorry to bother you, folks," Janan said. "But, Harry and I came across a few photos and would like you to take a look at them." She pulled the glossy photos out of a large manila envelope and offered them to the family. Immediately, all three of them said, "That's Oreo!"

"Where did you get these great photos of Oreo?" Bonnie asked.

"Harry pulled them off the Internet," Janan said. "We thought the dog was Oreo, but we were not sure."

"Oh, for certain it's him," Edward said. "Look, you can clearly see his collar with the tags on it in this one." He handed Janan one of the photos.

"Oh my," Janan said. "I had not noticed that, myself. You cannot make out the name on the tag. However, you can clearly see that the collar is blue and that there are two tags hanging from it."

"Yes, one of them has his name on it," Bonnie said, "and the other is a St. Francis medal."

"Mommy, can we take these home?" Toby asked.

Janan looked at Harry, who immediately said, "I made several copies."

"You sure can, young man," Janan said as she handed the envelope to Bonnie.

"Mommy. When you and daddy buy me a puppy, I want him to look just like Oreo," he said. Then he thought for a moment and asked, "Daddy, would it be OK if we named our puppy Oreo?"

Everyone in the room laughed. "I don't see why not?" Edward said. He held up one of the photos. "I think this Oreo would be very pleased to have a little cousin named after him."

Janan asked Harry to get another set of the photos he prepared and meet her in Myra Mitchell's office. A few minutes later, they were both seated in front of Myra's desk.

"Nice to see you again," Myra said. "Something new?"

Harry pulled the photos out of another manila envelope and handed them to Janan, who, in turn, gave them to Myra. "Ever see this dog?" she asked.

"He is so cute," Myra said, looking at the photo carefully. "Looks like a little brown and white Shih Tzu to me." Then she paused and looked at Janan and Harry. "No. You are not going to tell me that this is the dog you are looking for, are you?"

"Yep," Janan said. "The one and the same. However, Harry pulled that photo from a TV film clip on a Hanford, Illinois evening news show."

"When was that?" Myra asked.

"A little over a month ago," Janan said. "There was an incident in a homeless camp next to the Hanford park and the dog ran away. The TV news stories associated with the entire homeless situation there, including the dog, clearly report that his name was Oreo."

"I know Hanford," Myra said. "It is a good five hour drive from here. If that is the same dog, how did he get here?"

"I have no idea," Janan said. "However, it is curious that it was just about a month ago the Ernst family was told little Toby might have to be put in hospice – his leukemia situation was that dire."

Myra looked at the photos of Oreo Janan gave her more carefully. There were several different shots of the dog: one of him sitting, another chasing a ball and still another showing him lying on the grass with a tennis ball in his mouth. "I know he was not one of our dogs," she said. "However, I may have seen him or at least a dog that looked very much like him.

"Where?" Janan asked.

"As you know, the hospital courtyard directly abuts the river where there is a river walk. I seem to remember recently seeing a woman with a couple of children sitting on one of the river walk benches and a little dog like Oreo sniffing around nearby. I just assumed that the dog belonged to the woman and kids."

"Could he have strayed into the dog park somehow?" Janan wondered.

Saint Oreo

"No, not a chance," Myra said. "There is a double gate he would have to pass through. I do recall, however, thinking how cute the dog was. It looked like he had just been groomed."

"It would be pretty remarkable if somehow the poor creature made its way over 250 miles from Hanford Illinois to Cranston," Janan observed.

Myra simply nodded her head in agreement.

***

Megan Kinlaw had just left the morning staff meeting that the Hanford Channel 7 news director customarily held with her producers, assignment editors and on-air news people. She returned to her office and noticed that there were several voice mails waiting for her. Most of them were routine messages and return call requests from her colleagues. However, one of them was from a Janan Taylor at the Cranston's Children Hospital in Kansas. The message said that Janan wanted to talk to Megan about a dog named Oreo. Curious, Megan chose that one to return first.

Janan introduced herself, told Megan how she found her through an Internet search and then explained why she called her. Janan said she thought they likely had a common interest – a little brown and white Shih Tzu called Oreo who seemed to have a remarkable effect on people. Then, Janan relayed the story about Oreo and how he may have positively impacted a young leukemia patient's will to survive so much that the boy was now in complete remission instead of being placed in hospice. Janan was careful, of course, to observe the Health Insurance Portability and Accountability Act (HIPAA)

64

privacy law which protected Toby and his parents from being personally identified in any way.

Megan's interest was sparked immediately. She took copious notes, asked Janan many questions and shared what information she had available about the Oreo incident at Hanford Heights. No, she told Janan, no one had seen Oreo since the night Brenda Hopkins sent him scurrying away for his own protection. Yes, she said, the community response to the attention given the Oreo incident did have a significant positive carry over effect. However, that now was waning since peoples' memories seem to be short. Still, she said, it seems clear that Oreo would remain something of a legend in Hanford and many people continued to honor his memory.

The two women agreed to keep in touch and to share any new information about Oreo that might develop. For Megan, however, the story Janan told her was just what was needed to spice up that day's evening news. In turn, Janan had no idea that her call to Megan was about to unleash a media firestorm.

Saint Oreo

Chapter Eight

The Reverend George Watkins, pastor of Our Lady of the Grove Roman Catholic Church in Hanford, parked his car in the garage of the parish rectory. He closed the overhead door and entered the house through the rear hallway leading into the kitchen. Reverend Watkins unbuttoned his clerical collar and went into his private quarters, where he took off his shoes and relaxed in his favorite recliner. On the way through the kitchen, the sixty-five year old priest grabbed a cold Yuenling lager from the fridge. He twisted off the top of the bottle, raised the lager to his lips and savored the medium-bodied flavor of the amber liquid. Then, he took the HDTV remote from the table next to his chair and clicked the TV on to Hanford Channel 7 to get the local news of the day. He almost spat out a mouthful of Yuenling when the first image that appeared on the TV was a blown up photo of the little brown and white Shih Tzu the homeless people occupying Hanford Heights named Oreo.

It was dinner time at the bishop's residence in Brookfield. Hedy Olson, one of the volunteer ladies who took turns preparing meals for the bishop, walked into the parlor where His Most Reverend Excellency John O'Connor was seated with his assistant Monsignor Carl Obermann and two members of the diocese finance committee, all who were the bishop's guest for dinner that night. Hedy announced that dinner was ready and requested that the bishop and his guests move to the dining room.

In the old days, the days when nuns wore somber black or dark blue habits, at least three nuns would have been assigned full-time to serve as housekeepers at the bishop's residence. However, so much changed over the past few decades. Among those changes has been the dramatic decline in the number of Catholic nuns in the United States, a decline of over 70% over the past 50 years. Moreover, very few nuns in the United States wear habits, these days. Most prefer ordinary street clothes and even fewer have any interest in serving as diocesan or parochial housekeepers.

"Your Excellency, the meatloaf is going to get cold and I have to leave early this evening," Hedy said, urging the men to continue their discussion over the dining room table. Just then, Monsignor Obermann's cell phone rang.

Obermann answered it and waved the others on. A couple minutes later, Obermann walked into the dining room and said, "Your Excellency, that was George Watkins at St. Andrew's in Hanford. He told me he was watching the Hanford evening news and thought you might want to tune in to Channel 7 if we can pick it up, which we can because it is on our local cable network, too."

"Good grief, Carl. What is the problem? Don't tell me there is another scandal," the bishop said with concern.

"Not exactly," Obermann replied. "However, it seems that little Shih Tzu named Oreo has reappeared. This time at a children's hospital in Cranston, Kansas."

"You're kidding," the bishop said, laughing. "What has the dog done now that is newsworthy?"

"I'm not sure," Obermann answered. "But George thought you might want to watch the local news."

Much to Hedy's dismay, all four men returned to the parlor where the monsignor had turned on the television. They arrived just in time to see Megan Kinlaw talking about how Oreo, the "miracle dog," mysteriously appeared in Cranston, Kansas five weeks after his disappearance from Hanford Park, just in time to help cure a little boy named Toby Ernst who was suffering from acute lymphoblastic leukemia (ALL). Megan was talking against a background video of the homeless at Hanford Park. The video showed the homeless playing with Oreo, a food truck bringing meals to them and a woman crying with joy as she held a wiggling dachshund that some claimed Oreo brought back to life after it had been hit by a car. There was no question that the broadcast was intended to make it seem that the dog Oreo was not simply coincidently on the scene of these incidents, but rather that he was the cause of them.

The bishop was concerned. "This is getting out of hand," he said. "The news media is attributing mystical powers to an animal and it seems that a lot of the public is believing it."

Hedy walked into the room in a state of frustration. "Your Excellency, what do you want me to do with dinner?"

"Hedy is right, gentlemen," the bishop said. "It is time to enjoy another of her excellent and much appreciated meals." With that, and much to Hedy's relief, the bishop and his guests moved back to the dining room. After the men were seated, the bishop said grace and then added, "Sorry for the earlier interruption, gentlemen. However, 'dig in.' We certainly are not going to let an animal ruin a pleasant evening."

Of course, that was before the bishop saw the national broadcast news right after dinner.

***

Janan Taylor was livid with anger. The entire day had been a nightmare for her. Now, after watching national news on a major broadcast network, she was even more upset. The evening Janan spoke with her, Megan Kinlaw broke the story on Hanford Channel 7, which was almost immediately picked up by national broadcast channels. Janan assumed her conversation with Megan would be considered an exchange of confidential information between two professionals. It never occurred to her that Megan might betray the confidentiality of the conversation and use what Janan told her for her own personal gain.

Much worse, despite Megan practically pleading to learn the identity of Toby and his parents, Janan was emphatic that HIPAA, the federal patient privacy law, prohibited the release of that information without the patient's consent. Somehow, however, Megan found out Toby's identity; probably not difficult for investigative reporters, Janan later reflected. As a result, Toby's parents had been plagued with requests for interviews by a variety of news media organizations. Janan's office had been likewise bombarded. What a mess!

***

Hedy's meatloaf dinner was a success, even if not gourmet. Who could argue with Italian style meatloaf with gravy, mashed potatoes and buttered carrots accompanied by a bottle of Tuscan Chianti. Coffee and a simple dessert, vanilla ice cream, was served in the parlor so that Hedy could clean up and leave a little early as planned. The other reason dessert was served in the parlor was so the bishop could watch his favorite national evening news. Noting that the bishop was preoccupied by something more compelling than determining the next fiscal year's parish assessments, the two finance committee members excused themselves, leaving the bishop and his assistant fixated on the unfolding news report about the lovable, miracle dog who, according to the report, reappeared out of nowhere to cure a young leukemia sufferer.

Both of the clerics were understandably incensed every time the news report used the words "cured" and "miracle." "To even suggest that an animal has the ability to effect a cure on a human being, or, for that matter, even on another animal, is an affront to the Lord," the bishop said righteously. Monsignor Obermann nodded in agreement. Then, it got worse. The news clip showed a scene in front of the Ernst home where, as the bishop later said, good-intentioned but grossly misguided well-wishers were holding a candlelight vigil. A teenager was holding an oversized blown up photo of Oreo. Two others held a poster that had Toby's name inside of the outline of a heart. Some held only candles. Most joined hands, swayed back and forth and began singing a popular adaptation of Psalm 104 titled, Brother Sister Creatures:

Huge and tiny beings
Each one part of our family
Hearing, smelling, seeing
Each one part of our family

Brother sister creatures of the ground
Brother sister creatures of the sea
Brother sister creatures of the air
Oh, I love my brother sister creatures

That was more than the bishop could take! He grabbed the remote from Obermann's hands, clicked off the TV and put the device back on the table. Then, he crossed himself and stomped off to his room saying to Obermann as he left, "Carl, come on over for breakfast tomorrow morning after Mass. I want to place a call to the archbishop."

***

A Catholic bishop is the authoritative interpreter of the ethical and moral guidelines of the Church. He has very broad authority to resolve questions about matters of faith in his diocese provided his decisions are consistent with the teachings of the Church. In addition, he is the administrative superior of the priests and deacons in his diocese.

Bishop John O'Connor could have issued a pastoral letter to the priests and faithful in his diocese in which he put to rest the matter of the "miracle" dog by declaring that any belief that the animal possessed supernatural powers was heretical. However, that edict would have applied only to his own diocese. Because the problem had now spread to at least one other diocese, Bishop O'Connor prudently thought he should take the matter up one level and engage the archbishop in Chicago. Archbishops outrank bishops, but seldom overrule their decisions.

Unfortunately, while the archbishop agreed that the entire matter about the dog was absurd, he did not share Bishop O'Connor's sense of urgency. Foolish things like this happen all too frequently these days, he told the bishop. He opined that in a little while, it would all be forgotten and that there were more important matters of faith and morals to be addressed. However, he recognized the primacy of Bishop O'Connor's authority in his own diocese and said he should do as he saw fit among his own flock.

Discouraged, Bishop O'Connor returned to Brookfield where, after some thought and prayer, he called Bishop Alan Baker of the Cranston diocese, an old friend of his from seminary days, to learn how he was handling the situation. Bishop Baker said that there was no real evidence the dog actually existed. The boy and his parents might have mistaken the animal for another dog or the dog could simply have been a figment of their hopeful imagination. In any event, Bishop Baker retorted laughingly, in his diocese he had decided to "let a sleeping dog lie." The pun was fully intended but not appreciated by his friend.

That is probably where the story would have ended; a poignant story about a little dog who just happened to be at the right place at the right time. And, whose cute, but very explainable canine behavior, positively touched the lives of certain people, just like so many other dogs and cats have done for their owners. But then, another incident occurred and this one had both national and international significance.

Chapter Nine

It was 4:00 am and the rusty 1983 Jeep Cherokee had just passed through the small pueblo of Guerrero in the Mexican state of Coahuila. The driver, a twenty-five year old Mexican named Eduardo, softly whistled a sigh of relief. He had made the trip many times and knew with some certainty that the *policía local*, local police, would not likely be patrolling the area for another hour or so. Normally, he would not be concerned about being stopped and searched, except for the inconvenience. If Eduardo ran into a police checkpoint, even when his car was loaded with *inmigrantes ilegales*, the *policía* would usually give a perfunctory glance at whatever phony documents the "illegals" were carrying and then demand the usual bribe or *mordida*. The current bribe for a routine traffic stop was 1,600 pesos, $84 US dollars.

However, today, in addition to a young woman and her child, there were two *mulas*, drug smugglers called mules, riding in the back of the Cherokee, each guarding a square-shaped backpack that likely held plastic-wrapped packages of cocaine laced with fentanyl worth many thousands of dollars. If Eduardo had been stopped, the *policía* would certainly have arrested the *mulas*, confiscated the cocaine and then divided up the spoils back in their Guerrero police station. They might or might not release the coyote and his human trafficking passengers for the standard *mordida*. It was no surprise, therefore, that

Eduardo was relieved when he passed through the darkened pueblo without incident.

Twenty minutes outside of Guerrero, Eduardo made a sudden right turn onto a rutted dirt road that seemed to lead to nowhere. A few minutes later, he drove the Cherokee down an arroyo and followed the dry creek bed north toward the Rio Grande River and the United States border. As the SUV bounced along the twisting, uneven path, the headlights of the Cherokee showed that other vehicles had also recently driven along the arroyo. No one in the Cherokee said a word, nor had they since leaving Nuevo Laredo almost four hours earlier. The only sound came from Maria Morales Lopez, a twenty-year old woman from Guatemala who was humming and caressing her three-year old son Dacio. The boy slept peacefully in her arms, totally unaware of his surroundings.

Maria was born and grew up in a small hamlet on the outskirts of Fraijanes, Guatemala. Fraijanes is located on a fertile plateau in the region of Lake Atitlan, one of Guatemala's three major coffee producing regions. The mountainous region produces a variety of coffee called Arabica Lavados that is harvested from December through March. Because the coffee beans of this variety are grown at high altitudes in rich volcanic soil, they ripen slowly, resulting in a complex flavor prized by coffee lovers worldwide.

At least half of the Guatemalan peasants who work on the coffee plantations are illiterate. However, the Jesuits, who brought Christianity to Guatemala in the 1700s, ran a school in Fraijanes that Maria was able to attend through the fourth grade. So, she had basic reading, writing and arithmetic skills. In addition, she was bilingual, speaking both Spanish and Mayan, her ancestral language. During harvest season, both Maria and her mother picked coffee beans on one of the plantations owned by a large regional coffee producer. Maria's father had worked on the same plantation. However, he was killed during Guatemala's bloody civil war shortly after Maria was born.

Because of Maria's educational skills, she was able to continue to work in the plantation's coffee processing and shipping facility for several months after the end of each harvest season. Unfortunately, like most peasant women in the region, Maria's mother, Felicia, found very little work after the season ended. Every day, she would leave her home before sunrise and take the colorful and appropriately named "Chicken Bus" from her hamlet to Fraijanes. If she was lucky, she found work sweeping the streets, cleaning the steps of the Catholic churches or at other odd jobs that paid a few Quetzals each day.

In a good day, Felicia would earn forty or fifty Quetzals, the equivalent of $5.00 to $6.00 U.S. dollars. This was not as good as the $12 to $15 dollars a day she could earn picking coffee beans during the harvest season. However, together with what Maria earned, it provided the family's necessities. Sadly, only one cent out of a $3.50 cup of Guatemalan coffee in a U.S. coffee shop ever worked its way back to the Guatemalan peasants who picked and processed the beans.

When Maria was seventeen, she became pregnant by a young man named Rico who worked with her on the coffee plantation. When the baby was born, Rico moved in with Maria and her mother in their two room, 500 square foot, wood slat house on a Fraijanes hillside. There was no indoor plumbing. A single electric line provided one overhead light in each of the two rooms. Cooking was done on a wood burning stove made out of cemented river stones, which also provided heat during the cold season. Clothes were washed in a mountain stream and dried on a clothes line hung between two trees near the mother's house. For the most part, bathing was also done in the river, except at the coldest time of the year when it was dispensed with entirely. There was an outdoor latrine for toilet needs. Still, the interior of the house was neat and surprisingly decently furnished, considering the family's poverty status which was shared by the vast majority of their neighbors.

A year after baby Dacio was born, Rico heard about the migrant caravans that were forming throughout Central America and heading for the U.S. border. He told Maria that he planned to go to the United States to obtain work so they could have a better life. Soon afterward, he joined one caravan as it passed through Guatemala City. That was the last Maria heard from him for six months. Then, a neighbor, who had a cell phone, excitedly ran to Maria's house saying she received a message from Rico. He was fine and had found a job in Las Vegas working for a building contractor. He told Maria he would be home for Christmas and had a surprise for her.

As promised, Rico showed up a few days before Christmas. Maria thought he looked great. He presented Maria with her own cell phone and gave her and her mother five hundred U.S. Dollars. That was more money than either Maria or her mother had ever seen in their lives. Rico said he had made contact with some people in Mexico who help migrants slip into the United States, especially those joining one of the caravans. He said he would arrange for her to join another caravan that was being planned for the spring and would send her the money she needed to make the trip. Even though Rico was undocumented, he told Maria not to worry. There were plenty of people in the United States that help immigrants who were undocumented live happy, undetected lives.

So, Maria waited. She and her mother continued to earn a paltry subsistence and supplemented their income by tending a plot of corn on their property. Corn was the staple food in Guatemala. Tamales, tortillas, corn bread, corn fritters and *elotes locos* or crazy corn were all staples in the Morales-Lopez family diet.

In June of the following year, Maria and baby Dacio joined a caravan in Guatemala city and headed for the Texas border. Maria was terrified. She had never been away from Fraijanes before. Further, she was traveling with a three-year old and worried how she would care for him during the trip. Rico had prepaid his contact for each leg of the trip. In addition, he sent money to Maria to give to her mother until they could bring her to the U.S. and also money for Maria to take with her for travel expenses.

The caravan trip was remarkably uneventful. Although Maria found all of the talk and warnings about thieves, rapists and the like terrifying, she learned that the key was to stay with the people in the caravan you trusted. There was safety in numbers. Unfortunately, by the time the caravan reached Nuevo Laredo, Mexico, the United

States government had greatly increased border security and it had become much more difficult to slip across the border. Maria called Rico in a panic saying that the arrangement he made for them out of Nuevo Laredo had fallen apart. Rico, now in a panic, himself, hastily made arrangements with a coyote named Eduardo, who demanded twice the customary rate for the final leg of the trip. Rico had no choice except to pay the outrageous amount. However, he had to borrow from his friends in order to send the coyote the demanded payment.

Eduardo followed the arroyo for about a half hour. Then he stopped the Cherokee and told his passengers to get out. He told them his part of their trip was over and they were now on their own. Maria was stunned. She had expected that the coyote would escort her across the border into the US. However, all he did was pull a cheap foam lime colored noodle out of the back of the Cherokee and give it to Maria. "You will need this," he said callously. One of the two *mulas* saw the look of terror on Maria's face. He just laughed and told her to follow him and his partner. After Eduardo turned his Cherokee around and sped away, Maria set Dacio on the ground while she put her waterproof backpack over her shoulders. It was 5:30 am and the faint light of dawn was just beginning to be seen in the east.

Maria picked up Dacio and carried him with one arm while holding on to the noodle with her free hand. She followed the *mulas* down the arroyo until it abruptly came to a river. "The Rio Grande?" Maria asked. "Si," answered one of the *mulas*. The river would have been a formidable barrier to anyone crossing it except at this particular point a large sandbar covered with shrub stretched from within thirty feet of the Mexican side to more than half-way across the river. It was an easy wade in water barely knee high to reach the sandbar. On the other hand, at the northern end of the sandbar, there was a stretch of at least seventy-five feet of water of unknown depth.

Both of the *mulas* were from El Salvador. They did not particularly care for Guatemalans, particularly those of Mayan descent, which in Maria's case was obvious to them from her features and accent. Further, they had only one main interest: deliver the packs of cocaine to their U.S. contact, get paid and return to repeat the cycle over and over again. Nonetheless, the sight of a young mother with a small child elicited some compassion from them. The youngest said, "You do not need to know our names. Just follow us. We have done this before. The water here should not be higher than your chest. Use the noodle for the baby. And so, Maria and the two *mulas* began the last seventy-five feet of their journey to the United States.

As the young *mula* had said, the water depth of the river at that point did not get above her chest. However, at one point she slipped on something and went under for a moment. Dacio was fine because she had wrapped the noodle around his small body. Still, Maria was drenched when she got to the other side of the river and climbed up its muddy bank.

"Welcome to the United States!" the elder of the two *mulas* said. "Wasn't that easy?" Maria was bewildered. Now what, she wondered. Which way should she go? How would she get to Las Vegas? "Look, this is not our problem," the youngest drug smuggler said.

"No one forced you to come here. We have to leave and we will be traveling too fast for you to follow. Watch which way we are headed and then follow in that direction. Eventually, the US Border Patrol will pick you up and take you to a detention center."

"They won't hurt you," the other *mula* said. "In fact, because you are traveling with a child they will take good care of you and the baby and even allow you to call your husband. You will be fine."

Then the two *mulas* took off at a fast pace. Maria tried to follow their direction, but the terrain was so thick with large mesquite trees and brush that she lost sight of them within a few minutes. The sun had just risen above the horizon and Maria now looked out at a flat, tree and brush-covered landscape that seemed to merge endlessly into the horizon. Back in the Guatemalan highlands, she was accustomed to use mountain tops, plateaus, lakes and even neatly laid out coffee plantations as geographical reference points. Here it was impossible to do that; the land was too flat and the expanse was too broad.

Maria collapsed in a heap and sobbed. She clutched Dacio tightly because he was crying, also. Then, it occurred to her that the baby must be thirsty and hungry. She cleared a spot under a mesquite tree just above a shallow arroyo where she could safely put Dacio down. Next, she rummaged through her backpack for the few supplies she was able to bring with her. Most of the supplies were for Dacio: canned milk, bottles of water and jars of junior baby food. Even though he ate solid food, the baby food in jars was the best way to preserve food for him. There were also crackers, jerky and the inevitable corn meal in sealed plastic bags. In addition, Maria had packed one change of clothing for each of them, a few sanitary items, a photo of Maria's mother, another of Rico and several religious items, including a rosary. There was also a pack of matches in a waterproof case and her cell phone. Maria took the cell phone out of the backpack and turned it on. She was upset to see that the battery level was down to eighteen percent. Worse yet, she was apparently in a dead spot because there was no indication of a cell phone signal.

Replacing the cell phone in her backpack, Maria gathered some rocks from the bottom of the arroyo and place them in a circle. She collected a few pieces of the abundant deadwood near the tree, mounded them inside the circle of rocks and lit a fire. She mixed bottled water with a little canned milk and gave it to Dacio to drink. Then she opened a jar of Gerber mixed vegetables and gave that to him. Next, she changed into her only other set of clothes and spread her wet blouse, jeans and underthings over bushes to dry in the heat of the fire. Lastly, she took a little of the cornmeal, made it into a tortilla and baked it on a rock facing the fire. That would be her first meal of the day.

Dacio seemed to be having a great time. He had no idea he and his mother were in danger. Maria knew, however, she was lost. The sun had been up for over an hour and the temperature was rising. She tried to recall exactly where the sun rose – that would be east. Using a stick, she drew a line in the rough soil from her campfire in the direction she recalled seeing the sun when it first rose over the horizon. That became her east-west line. North and south were perpendicular to the line she had drawn.

A resourceful woman, Maria's plan was to trek due north, continuously moving away from the Rio Grande. She prayed her route would intersect a highway or that at least she would stumble on a ranch or farm. In either case, she was sure she would find someone to help her and Dacio.

While Maria folded her dried clothes and returned them to her backpack, Dacio played, chasing geckos. After stamping out the fire she built, she turned to pick up Dacio; but he was gone. A sick feeling overcame her. She screamed his name, but did not even know in which direction to search for him. Then, she heard him cry out in fright, followed by the loud, sharp bark of a dog. Running in the direction of the noise, she came upon a terrifying scene. Dacio was seated on the ground screaming. No more than fifteen feet away from him, stomping the ground, was the orneriest looking tusked feral hog she had ever seen. However, between the hog and Dacio was a little brown and white dog that was barking fiercely, clearly protecting the boy.

Maria slowly made her way to Dacio, not wanting to do anything to make the feral hog charge. She picked her son up, clutched him to her and slowly backed away. Meanwhile, the little dog became more aggressive and actually charged the hog, which apparently decided it had enough of the dog's insolence because it turned tail and disappeared into the brush. As soon as it was certain that it had successfully intimidated the hog, the little dog strode over to Maria, wagged its fluffy tail and cocked its head, as though it was giving her a thorough look over. As Maria carefully put Dacio down on the ground, her giggling son reaching out to pet the animal. It was then that Maria noticed the two tags hanging from the dog's

84

blue nylon collar. One was a medal with the image of St. Francis of Assisi, patron saint of animals. The other was in the shape of a dog bone with the engraved name Oreo.

Maria was buoyed up by her encounter with the little dog. She had no idea what breed it was nor did she care. She was imply grateful that the dog apparently protected Dacio from harm by chasing off the feral hog. Besides, the dog was cute and Dacio seemed to be fascinated with the little creature. Moreover, it was a domestic animal, which meant that it had to belong to somebody not too far away. That meant a farm or ranch must be nearby. But, where? She called the dog by the name on the tag hanging from its collar, "*Oreo, ven aquí, Oreo,*" beaconing the dog to come over to her. However, the dog simply sat and looked at her, as though it was puzzled. Suddenly, it occurred to her. She spoke to the dog in Spanish. What if the dog's owners spoke only English? Maria did not speak a word of English. How would she be able to communicate with the dog?

Then, without any prompting, the dog stood up and began walking in what Maria thought might be a northwest direction. She was afraid the animal would run away, cutting off the only lifeline she had. But, after a few feet it stopped and turned toward Maria, as though waiting for her to follow him. She slung the backpack over her shoulders, picked up Dacio and began walking toward the dog. As she approached him, the animal once again turned and walked a few feet ahead of her. It stopped, turned again and waited for her to catch up. Then it kept repeating the routine until it was clear the dog was leading her somewhere. "OK, Oreo," Maria said aloud in Spanish.

"I don't know whether you understand me or not, but I don't know what else to do. So, lead on!"

They walked for about an hour. The terrain slowly became more arid giving way to mostly scrub brush , occasional tuffs of grass and a few shorter mesquite trees here and there. Carrying Dacio became an almost impossible burden for Maria, especially as the heat of the day became more intense. Whenever, she faltered and had to sit down, Oreo walked back to her and whined or barked, as though trying to encourage her to continue.

The heat was now fierce and both Maria and the baby were sweating profusely. It was not long before she gave Dacio the last of the water she had brought with her. Then, shortly after she discarded the plastic bottle, Oreo came to an abrupt stop. In front of them, barring their path, was a wide irrigation ditch. There was no way to cross it safely; the sides were too steep and the water depth was unknown. Maria was in tears. Dacio was crying and wiggling to be put down. Oreo barked and began walking parallel to the ditch, still in a northwest direction. It was then that Maria heard a noise overhead. She looked up and saw a helicopter.

Chapter Ten

The U.S. Customs and Border Protection (CBP) is a federal law enforcement organization within the U.S. Department of Homeland Security. Air and Marine Operations (AMO) is a sub-organization of CBP. One of the branches of AMO is located at Uvalde, Texas, where the unit is responsible for patrolling 200 miles of the United States border with Mexico.

It was 11:00 am. The Huey II helicopter piloted by Jerry Garcia was twenty minutes into its two hour mission. Garcia and his copilot, Tom Williams, were both AMO Air Interdiction Officers (AIO) based in Uvalde. Their task was to spot any unlawful movement of people, including the movement of illegal drugs or other contraband, across the Rio Grande River into the U.S. If they spotted suspicious activity, they would inform CBP officers patrolling on the ground who would interdict any unlawful entries.

Both Garcia and Williams had served in Afghanistan flying helicopters; Garcia had served in the Marines and Williams in the Army. Rank in CBP was somewhat less formal than it was in the military. Garcia was three years senior to Williams and held the federal pay grade of GS 13. Williams, a more recent CBP recruit, was hired as a GS 11. The main difference between the two pilots was that Garcia earned over $75,000 while Williams' pay was about $58,000.

The Huey II was cruising at 1,000 feet altitude midway between the Rio Grande River and the extensive irrigation waterway that paralleled it to the north. So far into the mission, neither pilot had spotted anything except a few white tailed deer and an antelope or two. Then, Williams spotted something through the binoculars he held and said, "Hey bro, swing five degrees to the northeast. There might be something down there."

Garcia maintained altitude and speed and nudged the cyclic a little to his right. "What do you have, dude? Hope it's not another negative," he replied, using the CBP jargon that denoted a dead body. The previous day, they had spotted two negatives on the Mexican side of the river.

"Hell no, not this time," Williams said. "This one is wearing a pair of tight jeans that look like they were painted on her and she is waving like crazy." Garcia spotted what his partner was talking about and in one smooth, coordinated motion manipulated the aircraft's collective, throttle and cyclical to bring it into a hover.

"Hey man, nice ass," Garcia observed. "Whoa! Looks like she has a kid with her."

"And something else," Williams added. "Can't make out exactly what it is...maybe a jack rabbit. About twenty-five feet ahead of the woman and the kid."

Suddenly, the woman stopped waving. She put the child down, took her backpack off and sat on it putting her head in hands. "Damn, she's crying or something," Williams said. "And that animal is closing in on her."

"We better call base and have them send somebody out to interdict her," Garcia said. Then, the woman looked up, pointed to her mouth and to child's mouth and held her hands as if in prayer.

"Oh crap, she's pleading with us," Williams said. "I think she's trying to tell us she needs help."

Garcia was on the radio speaking with CBP base in Uvalde. "Base says it will be over an hour before they can get here," he told Williams. "Hey! What's that animal doing?"

"Looks like the damn thing is charging them," Williams answered. "Bro, maybe we better get this chopper down there."

When Maria first saw the helicopter she felt an overwhelming sense of relief. But then, it seemed like either whoever was aboard did not see her or were not planning to rescue her and Dacio. She tried to indicate to them that they had no more water and finally she pleaded with them in a way that transcended any language barrier. Even Oreo could tell Maria was in distress. He ran back to her, although there was nothing he could do except bark.

"OK dude, base just gave us permission to land on the basis that the woman is accompanying a child and they both might be in severe distress," Garcia said. "I am putting us down in that clearing about fifty yards from her." With that Garcia deftly cut back on the throttle, used the anti-torque pedals to keep the nose of the helicopter lined up with the woman and child below and set the craft down with scarcely a bump.

Garcia kept the turbine and rotor RPM at 68 percent while Williams jumped out and ran to the woman and child through a curtain of dust thrown up by the downdraft of the spinning rotor. Much to his surprise, the animal he spotted was not some kind of predator, but rather a small domestic dog. Williams took a bottle of water from the emergency pack he carried and handed it to the woman, who first gave it to the child before taking any for herself. Williams spoke almost no Spanish. However, he pointed to the woman and child and asked the universally understood "OK?" The woman nodded.

Williams picked up the woman's backpack and led her and the boy to the helicopter. Oreo followed, seemingly not at all happy with the noise, dust and confusion. Williams helped the woman board the helicopter and then passed the child and her backpack to her. He jumped into the open rear compartment, himself, and was about to signal Garcia to take off when both the child and Maria screamed "No!" They pointed to the dog who was cowering beneath the helicopter, trying to avoid the heavy downdraft from its rotor.

Williams spoke into his helmet microphone, "They want us to take the dog."

"Is it wild?" Garcia asked.

"I don't think so. It is brown and white with floppy ears and has a collar. Maybe it's their pet."

Garcia sighed, "Yeah, get it."

Williams jumped down on the ground again. Much to his surprise, the dog came right over to within his reach. He quickly grabbed the animal's collar, bringing it closer to him and then scooped it up passing it to the woman. Then he climbed back into helicopter, secured the compartment door and buckled his passengers into their seats. He secured the dog to a cargo strap. Dacio was thrilled that the dog was going with them and gently petted the animal. Williams returned to the cockpit and in less than three minutes, Garcia had the Huey II's turbine RPMs at 6,400 and the rotor at 324 RPM. A moment later they were airborne.

As soon as the Huey II was airborne, AIO Jerry Garcia informed his copilot that Uvalde Base instructed them to drop the passengers off at Breveton Station and then continue their patrol. "They said the Uvalde detention center was over capacity and had no room for even one more migrant," Garcia explained. He asked Williams whether their passengers spoke English.

"I don't know about the dog," Williams quipped. "But the gal does not and, of course, neither does the kid."

"Smart ass," Garcia responded. "You have the controls," he told his copilot, indicating that the responsibility for flying the aircraft was now fully in the hands of Williams. "I'll go back and talk to her."

"She's terrified," Williams advised.

Jerry Garcia was fluent in both English and Spanish. His parents immigrated legally to the United States in 1992 from Cuernavaca, Mexico. Officer Garcia was born a year later in McAllen, Texas. From the time their son began talking, Hernando and Beatrice Garcia were determined that he would be raised to be 110 percent American. Learning to speak English was a first priority for all of the Garcia's, as was making it the primary language spoken in their home. The senior Garcia's made sure their son Jerry was also raised in the richness of their native culture, as well as in all things American.

Garcia unfastened himself from his seat belt and shoulder harness. He squeezed past Williams on his right and went into the small rear compartment of the helicopter. The moment he laid eyes on his female passenger he could confirm William's observation that she was terrified. Garcia leaned close to the woman and shouted loud enough to be heard over the roar of the turbine and the incessant 'whumpp, whumpp' noise made by the rotor overhead.

"Bienvenido a Estados Unidos, señora. ¿Cuál es tu nombre y el nombre de tu patojo?" Garcia asked, welcoming her to the US and asking for her name and that of her child. Although Spanish is the official national language of Guatemala, a large percentage of its population, like Maria and her family, are of Mayan descent and speak Yucatec Maya among themselves. Maria smiled when Garcia used the Maya word *'patojo'* for child instead of the traditional Spanish *'hijo.'* She was pleased he recognized her Mayan heritage and appreciated the courtesy.

"My name is Maria Morales Lopez," she replied in Spanish. "My son's name is Dacio."

"Who is that little critter curled up at your feet?" Garcia asked.

"Ah, el pequeño perrito." She pointed to the tag hanging from his collar and said, "The little puppy's name is Oreo!"

Garcia then proceeded to ask Maria where she was from, how she got into the United States, where she was going and the usual initial questions asked of most migrants interdicted by the CBP. He told her not to worry; that she would be treated well and that she would not be separated from Dacio. Then he returned to the cockpit, took over the controls of the Huey II and a few minutes later landed at Breveton Station. The one question he failed to ask was whether the dog named Oreo belonged to her. He simply assumed it did.

Barely fifteen minutes later, Garcia set the Huey II down on a helipad in front of the main building at Breveton Station. A female Customs Border Protection officer, who introduced herself as Melinda Pérez, met the helicopter, took Maria and Dacio in custody and escorted them to the detention center's newly expanded processing facility. Curiously, the CBP officer took no particular notice of Oreo who followed the trio to the office building, briefly stopping when he found something interesting to sniff. When they reached the processing center, Oreo slipped into the building without notice, following Officer Pérez, Maria and Dacio through the automatic door.

Saint Oreo

Chapter Eleven

Breveton, Texas (population 1,500) is located on State Route 277 between Carrizo Springs and Eagle Pass in Maverick County, only twenty-two miles north of the Rio Grande River and about seventy miles east of Del Rio, Texas. The town was named after George Brevet, an early Texas pioneer who supplied cattle to U.S. Cavalry and Texas Militia outposts along and near the Rio Grande River. In past times, Breveton's economy was largely dependent on the local military population, including families of the troops. Now, Breveton is a decaying town serving area ranches and farms. Its main attraction, if it can be called that, is the U.S. Customs Border Patrol Station and detention center a mile south of town.

Not long ago, the Breveton CBP Station had fewer than fifty agents and officers. The original design and staffing of the facility was perfectly appropriate for its planned purpose. Then, the caravans began arriving from Central America, bringing thousands of migrants to the U.S. border, including many family and unaccompanied minor groups. Now, over one hundred agents and officers operated in and out of the station.

Unfortunately, like CBP facilities throughout all of the southern border states, Breveton Station simply could not effectively deal with the overcapacity crisis forced on it by the failure of the United States Congress to face up and deal with the border situation. The station's detention facilities were designed for perhaps thirty to forty people, mostly men who were suspected of illegally crossing the United States – Mexico border smuggling drugs and other contraband. However, because of the incredible number of migrants illegally entering the United States, the facility had been expanded to handle up to 250 men, women and children, who were supposed to be processed within a few days and then moved to larger more accommodating facilities. Breveton Station also served as a Federal Emergency Management Agency (FEMA) storage facility for supplies and equipment needed in the event of a natural disaster. Two FEMA employees were assigned to the Breveton Station to inventory and maintain those supplies.

Most of the CBP agents and officers at the Breveton Station, including Officer Melinda Pérez, spoke fluent Spanish. That was not surprising since over ninety percent of those entering the U.S. illegally along the Texas border were of Hispanic descent. Not all illegal migrants were Hispanic, however. Recently, there had been a small, but increasing, number of illegals from Southeast Asian, Middle East and African countries. Migrants interdicted from those countries were usually immediately sent to a larger CBP processing station that had appropriate translators available.

Officer Pérez was neatly dressed in the standard CBP summer uniform: dark navy blue slacks, short-sleeve shirt with distinctive CBP shoulder patches and a pair of plain black epaulets. The absence of a single silver stripe on her epaulets indicated that her pay grade was either a GS-5 or GS-7. A dark brass badge with the word "Officer" in the bottom rocker clearly indicated her law enforcement authority. After offering Maria and Dacio water, food and telling her where the toilet facilities were, Officer Pérez politely directed Maria and Dacio to an interrogation room and asked her to be seated. Dacio was fidgety and cried a little, so Maria had to hold him. Then, Officer Pérez took out some forms and began to question Maria about her background, the reason why she wanted to come to America and with whom she had contact during her travel from Guatemala. The interview lasted an hour and when it was finished Maria was exhausted and more frightened than ever.

Meanwhile, Oreo roamed the facility at will until a CBP officer named Charlie hollered, "Hey, what the hell? Who let that dog in here." Until then, apparently anyone who saw Oreo assumed he belonged to one of the other agents or officers. Now, unfortunately, Oreo became the focus of attention in a less than positive way.

"Thought it was yours, Charlie," another officer said. "Pablo, is it yours?" CBP Officer Joan Elliott asked another officer.

"Not mine. Maybe it belongs to Sam. Is the critter yours, Sam?" Pablo hollered.

"No," Sam said. Then he stood up from his desk and tried to corral Oreo. That was just what Oreo needed. Play time! Oreo loved running and chasing things and being chased himself. Soon, it seemed half the agents, officers and staff in the station were chasing Oreo, trying to catch him. But the nimble, little creature eluded them by slipping under chairs and desks, running right through their legs, or every once in a while wiggling out of hands that tried to get a hold on him. He practically tripped a woman staffer who was carrying a neat stacked of reports, making her fling the reports in the air where they fell to the floor in total disorder.

In truth, just about everyone was having fun! For the first time in a very long time, the on-duty staff of the Breveton Station momentarily forgot about the more somber aspects of their mission and relaxed. Actually, the moment of levity was almost like children having fun at school recess. Then, Oreo ran down one hallway and came to a screeching halt on the slippery floor tile in front of a shiny pair of black shoes worn by a very tall man in a black uniform. Oreo looked up at the 6' 6" man who had a Homeland Security Patch over his left shirt pocket with the initials FEMA in gold emblazed underneath. The man's black baseball cap also had the initials FEMA emblazoned on it. Roy Jones, one of two FEMA Emergency Management Specialists assigned to the Breveton Station, looked down at Oreo with his arms crossed. He must have made an intimidating sight to the fourteen pound dog because it was clear that Oreo did not like what he saw. Oreo spun around and began to run when in a commanding voice Jones said, "Stay!" Oreo stopped short and turned to look at Jones, who then smiled and said "Come!"

Oreo reluctantly returned to his original position in front of Jones and stood looking up at him until Jones said, "Sit!" Oreo complied. Jones reached into his right front pocket and pulled out a chewy chicken flavored dog treat that he threw down to Oreo who just looked at it until Jones said, "Okay!" Immediately, Oreo devoured the treat.

"I always keep a few of these in my pocket," Jones explained to the amazed onlookers. "This dog is no stray. When I was stationed in New Orleans, I trained and handled comfort and therapy dogs. My guess is that this little Shih Tzu has been trained either as a comfort dog or more likely as therapy dog."

"What's a Shih Tzu?" one of the female CBP officers asked.

"A Shih Tzu is a brachycephalic (squashed face) dog with naturally floppy ears. It's ancestry can be traced back to a long ago Chinese dynasty that bred the animal to be a combination watch dog and companion to Chinese emperors," Jones said.

"What is the difference between an therapy dog and a comfort dog?" asked another officer.

"A comfort dog, also called an emotional support dog, provides owners who need emotional support with therapeutic benefit through their companionship," Jones explained. "A therapy dog provides comfort and affection to people, including children, who might be in hospitals, hospices, disaster area centers, schools and nursing homes."

"How do you figure he is one of those therapy dogs?" someone asked.

"It is the way he responds to my commands. Those are the same commands typically used with therapy dogs. All I need is a little time with him and I'll find out for sure. Be back in an hour," Jones said, as he wheeled around. He gave the command "Heel!" to Oreo, who obediently walked directly next to Jones on his left side as the FEMA

Specialist walked out the back door of the processing center building.

**

When Officer Pérez completed her interview with Maria, she escorted her and Dacio through the CBP processing center into the facility's courtyard. The word courtyard was now a misnomer. All of the space in what had previously been an open area had been filled with tents, modular structures similar to temporary classrooms and mobile units. Breveton's interior detention facility was reserved for male detainees, including those with prior criminal records and other bad apples like MS-13 members who tried unsuccessfully to slip across the border. The border area where the *mulas* and Maria crossed was one of the few area in that region that lacked an effective fence or wall. Unfortunately, that area was well-known to human and drug traffickers.

Luckily, Maria was spared having to pass through the male detention area. Had she done so, she would have been subject to obscene cat calls, detainees exposing themselves to her and Dacio and a terrible stench that existed mainly because most of the male detainees could not care less about personal hygiene. Many simply relieved themselves through the retaining wire screen onto the hallway even though several toilets and a ten-person shower facility were available within the chain link fenced confinement area.

The detention area where Officer Pérez took Maria consisted of a series of six white Quonset type tents, each measuring 32' X 20'. Four of the tents were equipped with enough double bunk beds to comfortably accommodate

100

twenty people – five double bunks on each side with a five foot corridor down the center. Each double bunk had a four inch foam mattress, sheets, blanket, pillow and pillow case and a footlocker in front in which the detainee could store personal items. Maria and Dacio were assigned to a vacant double bunk that was located half-way down the corridor on the right side of the tent. Maria chose the top bunk and placed Dacio in the lower one.

The tent was brightly lit by sunlight passing through the fabric during the day and a lighting system running along the ceiling at night. Lights were dimmed, but not turned off, from 10:00 pm through 6:00 am. A circular fabric ventilation tube ran the length of the tent next to the lighting system. The tube provided air conditioning to the entire tent, maintaining a constant interior temperature of seventy-eight degrees. Ingress and egress to the tents was by way of a sturdy fabric flap built into each end that could be zippered if necessary.

Two of the tents were set up with tables, chairs, a small canteen dispensing water and other non-alcoholic beverages and snacks. There were two flat screen TV sets, one at each end of the tents, and a play area for children. There was also a table in each tent where free telephone calls could be made anywhere within the USA or to several international locations. Several cell phone charging stations were on the same table. This was the only interior area where detainees could congregate. Meals were brought in to this area three times a day on carts. There was a small grassed recreational area outside the tent complex with a children's play set consisting of swings, slides and climb bars. This was next to two mobile hygiene units. One of the units had showers for a half-dozen women or children at a time while the other had several toilet stalls and sinks.

Maria's impression as she first saw where she and Dacio would be detained for up to twenty days was that although restrictive, it provide facilities that were in many ways superior to what existed in her mother's house in Guatemala. What bothered her, however, was the very somber, depressed atmosphere she saw among the other women, including those with children. Women were sitting around practically lifeless as though they had given up hope. Children were sitting on the floor trying to amuse themselves, but more likely than not, they wanted to be held and comforted by their mothers. Later, Maria learned that was partially because some women had learned they would be deported back to their original countries. Others were still waiting for information about whether they would be deported or released pending later trial by an immigration judge. But, all-in-all, it was a gloomy sight.

***

FEMA Specialist Roy Jones, strode back into the main CBP office building with Oreo now on a leash. In a loud voice he said, "OK. Listen up everyone. We have ourselves a certified therapy dog."

"How about that," an agent named Sofia said. "How did that come about?"

"Well, I put the little guy through all of the paces that are required to certify a therapy dog. He passed with flying colors. That means he has previously been trained and certified."

"What was a therapy dog doing down by the border with a newly arrive migrant?" another agent asked.

"I do not have a clue," Jones answered. "I can tell you that it is highly unlikely he is from this area. The nearest hospital or other facility that might use therapy dogs is in Del Rio over thirty miles from here."

"Route 90 into Del Rio goes right pass here," CBP Officer de Leon observed. "Maybe he jumped out of a car or something like that."

"Yeah, maybe," Jones replied. "But, it's really strange, though. There is not a ranch or a farm anywhere near where the woman was apprehended. And, they were a good eighteen miles from Route 90 or any kind of state or local road."

"What are you going to do with him?" Sofia asked.

"He has no real ID," Jones said. "There is a tag hanging from his collar with the name OREO on it. But no telephone number or address. There is also a religious medal for pets – a St. Francis medal. Lots of people, especially Catholics, Episcopalians and Anglicans put that kind of medal on the collars of their pets. Any suggestions?"

CBP Officer Andrea Curtis spoke up, "Let's put a notice out in town about a found dog. In the meanwhile, since you say he is a trained therapy dog, I know just the place for him."

"Where is that?" Jones inquired.

"I think he will be a big hit in the women's and children's units," she replied. "The atmosphere is gloomier than death when you walk in there. He might just be the perfect way to brighten that bunch up!"

Supervisory Patrol Agent Pablo Hernandez was among those listening to Roy Jones's report about Oreo. "Sounds good to me," he said. "Andrea, why don't you and Melinda take Oreo out to the women's detention area and see how they respond to the little guy."

Jones told the women, "I'll fill you in on some simple commands for the dog later. Don't worry, he is gentle as a lamb." Then, he handed the leash to Officer Pérez and the two women led a very eager Oreo out to meet some new friends.

Maria sat at a table in the first dining tent with a woman from Honduras named Lucia. Dacio and a couple of other children were around the tables chasing each other. Neither Maria nor Lucia seemed interested in what the children were doing; both seemed preoccupied with their own thoughts and concerns. The same sense of discouragement prevailed among most of the other mothers and single women who were in the tent with them. The mood was slightly better among the children who, like children everywhere, usually seem to be more resilient than the adults.

There was a minor commotion at one end of the tent as CBP Officers Curtis and Pérez walked inside preceded by Oreo. Dacio immediately spotted the dog and shouted out, "¡Mamá! Oreo está aquí." Startled, Maria looked up and then broke out into a broad smile when she saw the little Shih Tzu. Lucia, the Honduran woman who was sitting next to Maria, also looked up. She shouted to her daughter Ana, who was sitting at another table, "¡Ana *mira! Un pequeño perrito,"* calling the girl's attention to the little dog.

Soon, the entire tent was in an uproar as children and adults, alike, gathered around the two CBP officers and the small brown dog they brought into the tent. For his own part, Oreo seemed to thrive on the attention. His fluffy little tail was wagging non-stop and every now and then he would bark with excitement that made the children laugh and clap their hands in approval.

"What do you think, Andrea? Is it safe to take him off the leash?" Officer Pérez asked her partner.

Andrea Curtis smiled and said, "I don't see why not. Like Roy said, he seems to be gentle as a lamb."

Melinda Pérez unfastened Oreo from his leash and turned him loose. Mayhem broke out as Oreo ran around in circles entertaining everyone in the room. The two CBP officers let Oreo play with the family groups in the first dining tent for a half-hour and then took him to the second tent where he was equally well received.

"I don't know how long this is going to last," Melinda said to Andrea. "But, if we can keep this little pup around for a while he will make our job a lot easier."

The little dog was doing what none of the CBP staff had been to achieve. His presence and antics helped to uplift the spirits of the female detainees and their children and take their minds off their plight – at least for a little while.

Saint Oreo

Chapter Twelve

Soon, word about Oreo spread beyond the boundaries of the Breveton Customs and Border Protection facility. The detainees had unrestricted use of their own cell phones and also had free access to landline phones in each of the two dining tents. They were in frequent contact with their loved ones and friends in places like Guatemala, Honduras, El Salvador, Nicaragua and, of course, Mexico. It was not that Oreo was doing anything exceptional. Rather, it was simply that his presence and interaction with the detainees and their family groups was calming and entertaining. It comforted them and even gave them a sense of affection. They were very grateful for his presence among them.

Maria was among the first to tell someone outside of Breveton Station about Oreo. She called her husband Ricco on her cell phone even as Dacio was playing with the dog. It was reassuring to hear Ricco's voice and to let him know she and Dacio were alright. Dacio excitedly told his father about the little dog named Oreo who lives with them. He also tearfully told his *papá* that he loved him and missed him and asked when *papá* would come to take him and *mamá* home. Ricco warned Maria not to tell any of the Border Patrol officers where he was, fearing they would send ICE to arrest and deport him.

Unfortunately, none of the detainees were aware that the international telephone calls they made might have been recorded by a certain intelligence agency that was monitoring calls for purpose of interdicting the smuggling of illicit drugs and human trafficking. Nonetheless, within only a few days, the social media in the seven Central American countries plus Mexico and even the U.S. border states began to take notice of a benign, but unusual, event that was taking place at a Customs and Border Protection station in Breveton, Texas – an event that centered on a small dog named Oreo.

***

FEMA Specialist Roy Jones was concerned that there had been no response to the "Found Dog" postings made on the station website and at several places in town. It was his idea to keep Oreo at the station and use him as a therapy dog, but only temporarily. As successful as the idea had thus far been, the question of the animal's ownership remained, as did the fact that he could not be kept at the station as some sort of mascot for long. Jones was passing by the desk of CBP Officer Lennie de Leon, who was staring intently at the computer screen on his desk, when de Leon suddenly swore and said, "Will you look at this!"

"What do you have, Lennie?" Jones asked. "Anything FEMA related?" Jones knew that if it was not FEMA related it was none of his business. He was surprised when de Leon said, "I don't know. Maybe."

Jones looked at de Leon's computer screen. A full size, full color picture of a dog that looked very much like Oreo stared back at him. "What the hell?" he muttered.

"Roy, just on a whim, I decided to put Oreo's name in the browser search bar. I wondered if perhaps his owners had posted a 'lost dog' message somewhere. But, this is incredible!"

De Leon's loud comments had attracted the attention of other nearby officers and agents, who now gathered around his computer screen. Soon they were joined by Supervisory Patrol Agent Pablo Hernandez. What unfolded on the screen was the complete story of a so-called 'miracle dog' that began in a municipal park in Hanford, Illinois and continued at a Children's Hospital in Cranston, Kansas. Everyone was dumbfounded at what they read. But, that was not the end of it. The search results were filled with references to a Shih Tzu named Oreo, many of them suggesting that the dog had been spotted in other areas. One report said that a dog matching Oreo's description was seen in a small town on the shore of Lake Erie after a storm rescuing a female cat and her litter from flood waters. Another report from a mother in Florida, claimed a dog looking like Oreo killed a venomous snake that was threatening her child.

And so the reports continued: Bakersfield, California; Anniston, Alabama; Keene, New Hampshire; Cumberland, Maryland and other U.S. locations. In all cases, the dog was seen doing something heroic or benevolent. Perhaps not surprisingly, the more recent reports came from south of the border, from cities and towns in Mexico and Central America: La Rosita, Nicaragua; La Palma, El Salvador; Flores, Guatemala and more. Interestingly, most of the Central American cities and towns in which Oreo or his clone supposedly appeared were the starting points for some of the migrants now detained in the Breveton facility.

"I have no idea what the meaning of this is," Supervisory Patrol Agent Hernandez said. "However, find that dog and bring it to my office immediately."

CBP Officer Melinda Pérez quickly rounded up Oreo and took him to SPA Hernandez's office as ordered. FEMA EM Specialist Jones accompanied Pérez because he seemed to have the greatest knowledge about the dog and its various characteristics. CBP Officer de Leon was present with several screen prints and other reports he downloaded from his computer. Hernandez sat behind his desk looking completely befuddled. Oreo stood in the middle of the office defiantly. He seemed to stare at the humans around him with an accusing look, as though he questioned why his playtime with the migrant children had been interrupted. Then, having apparently made his point, he walked around the room sniffing for something interesting.

"What the hell is going on here?" Hernandez asked the small group in front of him. "What am I missing? This is a dog, correct?" he asked for reassurance. "A plain ordinary dog." Everyone nodded in agreement. "Then, how is it possible all of these reports suggest that over the past ten days, this very same dog has been making the rounds of not less than seven countries – not to mention nine states here in America?"

His question was met with silence. Then, Roy Jones spoke, "Pablo, I have some experience with people who are in or who have been in high stress situations. In many ways, the psychological stress on people who are in hurricane and other disaster evacuation centers parallels that which many of the migrant detainees in our facilities are experiencing."

Hernandez interrupted Jones, "Yes, yes, however, it is not the migrants here who are attributing all of these events to your dog," he said emphasizing the word 'your.' It is people hundreds, if not thousands, of miles from here who are doing so."

"Yes," Jones agreed. "However, my guess is that almost all of what is being reported in the social media and on the Internet can be traced to telephone calls people in those areas received from migrants right here in this facility or from their friends and relatives who they previously contacted. Word spreads and so do unfounded rumors and wild stories."

Hernandez took a deep breath and exhaled. "You might be correct," he said. "Still, I am going to buck this up to the PAIC (Patrol Agent In Charge) and recommend that she forward it to the Section Chief in Del Rio. But first, contact our K-9 veterinarian. I want a complete examination of this dog to make sure it is a real animal and not something out of a science fiction novel."

"I don't think you have to worry about that, sir. Oreo is a real dog." CBP Pérez said decisively.

"Why do you say that, Melinda?" Hernandez asked.

"Because he just peed on your desk," she replied.

***

The Breveton Patrol Agent In Charge took one look at the report Supervisory Patrol Agent Hernandez sent to her, including the K-9 veterinarian's certification that Oreo was a real dog, and decided that the matter was above her pay grade. She concurred with Hernandez's recommendation that the situation be referred to the Section Chief in Del Rio. So, she signed the required referral form and sent the problem on its way to higher authority. It was no longer her problem.

Oreo was given a reprieve of sorts. He was allowed to return to the female detention tents so that he could continue to play with the migrant children and do what therapy dogs are supposed to do – give comfort and solace where needed. However, SAP Hernandez placed him under 24 hour watch, which meant that after lights out at 10:00 pm, he was put in a cage in the K-9 section. Previously, he had been allowed to remain overnight in one of the sleeping tents. Actually, due to Oreo's popularity, the female detainees had worked out an arrangement where his care was rotated among them. The adult women in each tent took turns making sure he was taken outside for his necessaries and also for ensuring that he was kept supplied with drinking water, dry dog food and treats.

The bad news that until further notice Oreo would be kept under close watch in the K-9 section at night was largely offset the next morning. Maria and her new friends Sofia and Lucia learned that because the immigration court dockets were completely overwhelmed, they were being released on their own recognizance pending notification of a trial date – probably two or three years in the future. All they had to do was keep immigration officials informed of their whereabouts. The colloquial term for that good news was called "catch and release." In any event, they were told that the next day a bus would take them to the section headquarters in Del Rio where arrangements would be made for them to join friends, sponsors or family members who were already in the United States. Maria was ecstatic that she would soon be reunited with her husband Ricco and that Dacio would soon see his *papá* again.

***

Miguel Reyes was a tough guy. He was a wannabe MS-13 gang member, but had not yet been initiated into his local gang, called Barrio 6. In order to pass initiation, Miguel would first have to kill a member of a rival gang and then he would have to undergo a beating by his fellow gang members while they slowly counted up to 13. The number 13 is of symbolical significance to MS-13 gangs. Miguel was twelve years old. A year ago, his brother Juan was brutally killed by members of Barrio 7. Juan's mutilated body was found on a roadside outside of Delgado, El Salvador, several miles from the Reyes rural home.

Miguel's mother, Sara, was a devout Christian. She did the best she could raising Miguel and Juan in a fatherless home, teaching them Christian values. For a while, Miguel was an altar boy at San Luis Catholic Church in Delgado. Like his brother, Juan, he had been baptized and had made his first Holy Communion. He had not yet received the sacrament of confirmation. If he joined MS-13, otherwise known as Mara Salvatrucha, he never would. Unlike his deceased older brother, Miguel had not yet given his body, soul and unquestioned loyalty over to the one of the most evil criminal cults in the world. His mother fervently prayed that God would spare him that fate. Then, as if in answer to her prayers, she learned that a caravan was being formed to take migrants from El Salvador to the United States where they could seek asylum.

Two months later, Miguel held the status of unaccompanied minor as he and a couple of friends joined the caravan and began the long, arduous trip to the U.S. border in Texas. At first, Miguel totally rejected the idea of leaving El Salvador and the prospective fellowship of the Barrio 6 gang. However, in reality, the economy in rural El Salvador was in such precarious condition that practically every day it was a struggle finding enough food to put on the table of their home, a shack made of plastic and corrugated sheet metal.

By comparison, the house owned by Maria Morales Lopez's mother in Guatemala was substantially better constructed and furnished than the Reyes home, as was the Morales-Lopez's overall standard of living. The poverty level of Miguel and his mother was the catalyst for his decision to join the caravan; that and the thought that once in the United States he might be able to travel to Los Angeles or Chicago and join a MS-13 gang in one of those cities. However, before he joined the caravan, he hugged his mother tenderly and promised to send for her as soon as he had saved enough money so that she, also, could have a better life.

In many respects, Miguel's travel with the caravan was much easier than Maria's. He did not have the burden or responsibility of caring for a small child while traveling. Further, he used his "tough guy," MS-13 façade to ward off most conflicts. Even adults were intimidated by his bravado and his frequent use of the MS-13 satanic hand sign. The gang symbols already tattooed on his body, including hands clasped in prayer meaning "mother forgive me for my crazy self" and the tattooed numbers 6 and 7, which together add up to the highly symbolic number 13, lent further credibility to the threatening image he intentionally projected. Unfortunately for Miguel, unlike earlier caravans from Central America, this one fell apart even before it reached Mexico City.

The first sign of trouble for the Central American migrant caravan was when Mexicans in the smaller towns across the border from Guatemala refused to provide the migrants with the same hospitality they had extended to earlier caravans. Earlier migrant caravans had been well received by the local populations they passed through or where they overnighted. Locals had set up food kitchens and provided reasonably comfortable overnight facilities for them. No more. The Mexican government was beginning to crack down on the caravans and, frankly, the Mexican people were beginning to tire of an endless stream of people from "south of the border" who many believed were straining local resources.

It was in the south central Mexican City of Puebla, about 100 kilometers south of Mexico City, that Miguel's caravan journey ended. The Mexican Federal Police broke up the caravan and dispersed the migrants. Some returned to their point of origin. Others tried to find work in Puebla itself or in Tlaxcala, Cuernavaca or Toluca – all cities within fairly easy reach from Puebla. Miguel and a handful of other El Salvadoran youths hopped a freight train and made it as far as San Luis Potosi, almost 500 kilometers north of Puebla, before being kicked off the train by the police. Soon, he was alone and frightened.

Miguel kept pushing northward relying on handouts from the locals in the towns he passed through or charity handouts from various churches and religious societies. A month later, hungry and exhausted, he found himself wandering the streets of Monterrey, Mexico – still over 200 kilometers from his destination, Nuevo Laredo, on the U.S. border. Miguel and other members of the caravan hoped that once they reached Nuevo Laredo, they would simply be able to walk across the port of entry bridge into Laredo, Texas where they would apply for asylum. As an unaccompanied minor, Miguel was certain that the U.S. Immigration authorities would readily grant his request. He was quite naïve. That was not how the system worked.

Freddie, the only name the sleazy man observing Miguel would acknowledge, studiously watched the boy approach business people shopping and going about their business in the Zona Rosa on the west side of Monterrey's Macro Plaza. From time to time, a passerby would reach into a pocket or purse and give Miguel a few pesos. The man noted that after Miguel received perhaps twenty or thirty pesos, he would stuff what looked like half into his pockets and then head off to find a street vendor from whom he bought an empanada or a gordita and a beverage. The man noted that the boy would then stuff any uneaten food into his backpack and return to entreat other passersby for more pesos. The man also took note of Miguel's tattoos, which were clearly MS-13 oriented.

As Miguel was stuffing several more pesos into his pocket, the man called Freddie flashed him the MS-13 hand sign. In fact, Freddie had nothing to do with MS-13. He was a flunky who worked for the Monterrey *Cartel Del Noreste*, the Cartel of the Northeast, that was in the process of wresting control of Monterrey's criminal enterprises from another cartel called the Zetas. Miguel was startled when he saw the sign that Freddie flashed. However, when the man motioned for Miguel to follow him, the boy did so eagerly. Freddie led Miguel to an apartment building in a less affluent part of Monterrey. He punched a code on a keypad to the left of the door leading into the apartments and, after a buzzer sounded, entered with the boy trailing close behind. Once inside, Miguel found himself surrounded by three of the meanest looking thugs he had ever seen.

They questioned Miguel for over an hour about his background, his relationship with MS-13 and the reason he wanted to go the United States. If Miguel made the mistake of engaging in "wise guy" talk, one of the thugs would slap him so hard across the face that blood trickled from his mouth. But in the end, despite his youth, they had a proposition for him. They would be happy to ensure that Miguel made it across the U.S. border if he agreed to deliver a package to a friend of theirs on the other side. It was that simple. Miguel readily agreed. He had no idea, nor did he care, what was in the package. He also did not know that once he delivered the package there was a good chance the recipient would slash his throat and leave his body to be found as another "negative" by a U.S. Customs and Border Protection patrol.

Saint Oreo

Chapter Thirteen

It was simply a coincidence that on the day Maria, Dacio and a few other detainee women and children were being transported to Del Rio, a very partisan congressional delegation was making an inspection tour of several U.S. Customs and Border Protection facilities in Texas. The United States Congress's failure to enact any remedy to the immigration crisis along the U.S. southern border hardly prevented its members, especially those up for reelection, from finding ways to sling mud and accusations at their opponents. The congressional delegation touring the Breveton facility were not really concerned about fixing the immigration problem. Rather, they were looking for anything that might be considered cruel and inhumane treatment of the detainees so that upon their return to Washington, D.C., they would be in an even better position to criticize members of the opposing party.

The delegation was small, consisting of only a half dozen congressional members; none of whom, interestingly, were from the State of Texas. In order to be politically correct, the delegation was divided equally between men and women and had a proportionate number of minority representatives. The Breveton Station senior staff had arranged for quite a "dog and pony" show for the delegation. Actually, the term was somewhat accurate in that several steeds used by the Border Horse

Patrol and a few K-9 dogs were put on display, as well as a little brown and white Shih Tzu therapy dog named Oreo.

While the congressional delegation was receiving a tour of the facility and attending perfunctory briefings, a CBP bus pulled into the station's front parking lot. The CBP officer driving the bus parked behind the chartered bus that had brought the delegation to the station. Engine still running, he got out of the bus, opened its baggage bays and then strolled over to chat with a buddy he spotted having a smoke outside of the processing center.

Meanwhile, accompanied by CBP officers Melinda Pérez and Andrea Curtis, Maria and the other detainees and their children who were being transported to Del Rio came out of the processing center and began boarding the bus. Oreo was there, too, so that the children could say goodbye to the little dog that had brought them such comfort. About the same time, the congressional delegation left the processing center and headed for their own chartered bus.

***

Earlier that day and some forty miles southeast of Breveton Station, Miguel Reyes learned that he was not the only person delivering a package to a "friend" of the Cartel Del Noreste thugs across the U.S. border. There were five other young men, but none as young as him. He had no way of knowing that the rusty 1983 Jeep Cherokee in which he was a passenger was the same one that barely two weeks earlier carried Maria Lopez, her son Dacio and two *mulas* down the same arroyo leading to the Rio Grande River. As when Maria traveled that route, the sun had not yet risen and Miguel had no idea where he was;

although, the earliest pre-dawn light was now becoming visible in the east. All he knew was that the driver's name was Eduardo.

The Jeep stopped suddenly and Eduardo ordered his passengers out of the vehicle. As soon as the sixth *mula* grabbed his backpack from the back of the Jeep, Eduardo spun the wheel and roared back up the arroyo the way he had come. Miguel had been briefed about how to cross the river at this point and followed the other *mulas* silently. They crossed a shallow part of the river onto the sandbar where Maria and Dacio had trod and then more gingerly waded across the wider stretch of the Rio Grande.

Within a few minutes they were back on dry land among a cluster of large mesquite trees. All six took off their backpacks and sat down for a short rest before beginning their trek to meet their contact a few miles away. That is when the entire area around them broke out in bright lights as a squad of U.S. CBP agents ran shouting into the clearing, guns drawn and pointed at the *mulas*. One of the thugs interrogating Miguel had been an informant. As a result, CBP agents were able to interdict the hapless *mulas* and prevent over a half million dollars' worth of heroin laced with fentanyl from poisoning the streets of America.

Miguel had never been more frightened in his life. He sat in the rear compartment of a hot CBP transport van, zip tied at his wrists and shackled along with the other *mulas* who had just been arrested. Suddenly, being a tough guy MS-13 wannabe seemed to be the stupidest thing he had ever done. It was all made worse when the older *mulas* began to taunt him.

"Hey *baboso*," one of the *mulas* shouted at Miguel, calling him something worse that a dumb person. "You got big problems now!"

"Yeah man," said another. "They gonna put you in *la pinta*, prison, for a long time. You never gonna see your mamma again."

Still another described in obscene and gruesome detail what kind of treatment Miguel was likely to receive from older male prisoners. It was all terrifying to him. He felt completely helpless and was on the verge of tears. However, there was no way he was going to let these animals see how scared he was. So, he gave them the universal sign for performing an impossible act, hung his head and for the first time in a long while began to pray.

At El Indio, a small town with a population of 263, the CBP transport van turned right on County Road 2644 and proceeded north toward State Route 277 and Breveton, now only sixteen miles distant. A second CAB van transporting the interdiction squad followed a hundred yards behind. Twenty minutes later, the prisoner transport van pulled into the front parking lot of the Breveton Station, while the van with the interdiction squad drove around the rear of the processing center.

***

Congresswoman Amy Kernan was accompanied by her Chief of Staff, Joseph Talbot as she and the other members of the congressional delegation headed toward the chartered bus that would take them to Del Rio where a military Boeing 737 was waiting to return them to Washington, D.C. The tour of the Breveton facility had been somewhat of a disappointment for the members of

122

the delegation. Contrary to their expectations, they found the detention accommodations for both men and women were clean, sanitary and humane – as was the overall treatment accorded to detainees as reported during random interviews with them.

A few problems were found, but none that would give the congressmen and congresswomen much additional mud to sling when they returned to Washington. If anything, there was ample evidence that the officers and agents of the U.S. Customs and Border Protection were doing a very credible job coping with Congress's failure to alleviate the overcrowding condition at the facilities they visited. Again, disappointing.

As the members of the congressional delegation and their staffs were approaching their bus, the two drivers of the prisoner transport vehicle and a third CBP officer began unloading the six *mulas* from the rear of the van. As wrist zip-tied and shackled Miguel stepped down onto the parking lot pavement, Congresswoman Kernan stopped short. She pointed to Miguel and in a voice loud enough for everyone in the area to hear, she said, "That young man. He's just a boy!" Then, she turned to her Chief of Staff and said, "Joe. Find out why they have him shackled and tied up like the older men."

Talbot quickly walked over to Supervisory Patrol Agent Hernandez and asked him why the boy was being treated like an adult. Hernandez told Talbot that Miguel was a mule, a drug smuggler and pointed out the MS-13 tattoos on his body. "He is likely very dangerous," Hernandez said.

Talbot reported back to his boss who became furious. "Does he speak English?" she asked. "No," replied Hernandez. "Just Spanish."

"Then, ask him how old he is," she said. Hernandez complied with her request. "He said he is sixteen," Hernandez said. "I don't believe it," Kernan replied. Then, she walked up to Miguel and in heavily accented Spanish asked, "What is your name?"

"Miguel. Miguel Reyes."

"How old are you, Miguel? And, do not tell me sixteen."

Miguel lowered his head. He must be in even bigger trouble than he imagined, he thought. "Twelve, *señora*. But I will be thirteen in October!"

Congresswoman Kernan turned back to Hernandez and said, "Immediately take those shackles off him and remove that plastic zip thing on his wrists. This kid is a minor, an unaccompanied minor at that."

Alerted that something interesting was beginning to happen, several congressional staffers began filming the scene on their cell phones. The detainees already on the CBP transport bus watched the unfolding scene with fascination; some using their cell phones to film what was happening. SPA Hernandez reluctantly gave one of the CBP officers the order to unshackle Miguel, but told the congresswoman that it was necessary to keep Miguel restrained by the plastic cuff until he was processed.

"Bullshit!" Congresswoman Kernan said angrily. She whispered to her Chief of Staff who reached in his pocket and gave her something. It was pocketknife. In a flash, the congresswoman flipped open the knife and grabbed Miguel's wrist restraint, cutting the plastic cuff as she said, "There! If you will not do it I ..."

She was cut short in mid-sentence as Miguel, now completely unrestrained, grabbed the knife out of her hand, pulled her by the hair toward him and put the knife to her throat. For an instant, everyone was in shock. Then, almost in unison, every agent and officer present reached for his or her handgun, cocked it and pointed it toward Miguel, who was now screaming incoherently in Spanish that he did not want to have to hurt anyone; that he wanted to go home; that he did not want to go to jail; and, that he was not a member of MS-13.

Miguel now had his left arm tightly wrapped around Congresswoman Kernan's neck, while he menacingly held the point of the knife against her throat with his right hand. The woman was in in a state of absolute terror. SAP Hernandez whispered to the officers standing next to him, "On my command take him out!" And then, as if on cue, Oreo pranced right up to Miguel and the congresswoman. He sat down, looked up at Miguel and barked playfully. He stood up on his hind legs, placing his front paws on Miguel's jeans, and began pawing, as though he wanted Miguel to pick him up.

Miguel looked down at Oreo and saw a look of pleading in the little animal's eyes - more than pleading. It was as though the dog was trying to convey a message to him – one of love, affection and acceptance. Miguel stared at Oreo for a moment. Then, he threw the knife away, released Congresswoman Kernan and reached down to pick up Oreo as he began sobbing. Oreo leaped into his arms and began licking the tears from his eyes. Officer Pérez rushed forward and put her arms around the terrified twelve year old.

"It's OK, Miguel," she said. "Everything will be alright. You are safe. I promise we will take care of you."

SPA Hernandez gave the order to stand down while CBP Officer Curtis joined her partner. Together, they consoled the still sobbing child and then gently led him into the processing center's main entrance. A very shaken Congresswoman Kernan staggered over to her Chief of Staff who tried to comfort her as she broke down and began to cry.

Less than an hour after the excitement ended, both the congressional chartered bus and the detainee transport bus were on their way to Del Rio; the first to the airport and the latter to the bus terminal where the detainees would be put on different busses for the next segment of their respective journeys. Back at Breveton Station, all of the CBP agents and officers involved in the confrontation were breathing a sigh of relief. Then, FEMA EM Specialist Roy Jones said, "By the way, where is Oreo?"

Pérez and Curtis looked at each other and shook their heads. Soon, there was a mad scramble as almost everyone searched both inside and outside of the building complex trying to find the little animal that unquestionably was the hero of the day. But, Oreo was nowhere to be found. Later, it was concluded that Oreo must have jumped into one of the open baggage bays of the detainee transport bus and ended up in Del Rio. However, when the driver of that bus was contacted, he said that no one at the Del Rio bus terminal saw him. If he had been in the baggage bay, the driver suggested, perhaps he slipped out while no one was watching.

A few weeks later, the sad and dejected staff at the U.S. Customs and Border Patrol Breveton Station framed a photo of Oreo and hung it on the same wall that contained an Honor Roll of fallen Breveton Station K-9 dogs. Along with them, he was greatly missed.

Saint Oreo

Chapter Fourteen

Fortunately no one from the news media was present to witness the debacle that unfolded at the Breveton Station that day. Immediately after Miguel was taken into the station's processing center, Congresswoman Kernan recognized the stupidity of her unlawful act. She practically begged her fellow congressmen to play down the matter. Since they had nothing to gain by publicizing the incident, they tacitly agreed to forget that anything much out of the ordinary happened. However, they apparently forgot they were not the only ones who witnessed the event; nor were they the only ones with camera apps in their cell phones.

The next day, Congresswoman Kernan was back in her office in the Longworth House Office Building in the Capitol Complex. In addition to being much embarrassed by the previous day's incident, she was also emotionally impacted by the experience, including compassion for Miguel Reyes and the hard, dangerous life he and his mother endured in El Salvador. The congresswoman took the incident up with the Secretary of Homeland Security who granted a waiver that dispensed with the usual processing time. Almost immediately Miguel was granted asylum. Further, because he was an under age 13 minor, no charges were brought by his desperate, impulsive act that, in the end, did not result in appreciable harm – except to the pride of Congresswoman Kernan.

Congresswoman Kernan also began the process by which Miguel's mother Sara would eventually be able to join him in the United States. Still, try as she might, she was not able to suppress all of the details of that day's events. After all, everyone knows that Congress, itself, is the most egregious leaker of information to the news media. The strategy of the "leakers," however, was to protect the congresswoman as much as they could and instead to focus the incident on how a little dog named Oreo mitigated what had been a looming tragedy.

In fact, Oreo's earlier impact on the women detainees at Breveton and their children had already begun to circulate within the social and news media, rekindling previous reports about the same little animal that arose in Hanford, Illinois, Cranston, Kansas and elsewhere. Yet, no one could imagine the international news firestorm that would unwittingly be unleashed by Sara Reyes, a religiously devout mother in the Central American country of El Salvador whose only fault was gratitude for the safety of her son Miguel.

After Miguel was processed for detention at the Breveton Station, he was taken to the unaccompanied minors section. This section consisted of one tent exactly like the four bunk room tents where female detainees and their small children lodged. Miguel was assigned a bunk, allowed to shower and was given both a wholesome meal and a clean set of clothes to wear. The clothes he arrived in were deemed not suitable for further wear and were summarily disposed.

Miguel was also given the opportunity to contact his mother, which was a problem because the poor woman did not own a telephone of any kind. So, with the help of CBP Officer Pérez, Miguel contacted Padre Tomas, the pastor of San Luis Catholic Church in Delgado, El Salvador. Miguel explained all that had happened over the past three months to the padre and asked him to let his mother know he was alright. In turn, the priest sent one of his assistant's to relay the message to Sara. The assistant also brought Sara a recent photo of Miguel taken at the detention center to prove he was in good health and an emotionally charged photo of Oreo giving comfort to him that was being widely circulated in the news media.

Miguel's mother was relieved beyond words. Later that day, she walked all the way to the church of San Luis, seven miles away, where she knelt before a beautiful, hand painted statue of Our Lady of Guadalupe, who was designated patroness of the Americas by Pope John Paul II in 2002. She expressed her gratitude in prayer and, as customary in many countries, placed the photo of her son Miguel at the base of the statue begging that the Virgin continue to protect him. Next, she did something very unconventional. She also placed the photo of Oreo at the base of the statue, expressing gratitude that the Lord sent such a blessed creature to console Miguel when he was in great anguish.

That weekend, an American tourist visited the church of San Luis and noticed the photos and messages left by devotees who were imploring the Virgin for various favors. The photos of Miguel and Oreo caught the woman's eye. She took a cell phone picture of stature with the photos and Sara's handwritten petition and posted it on Facebook. Within twenty-four hours, the photo went viral. A week later, there were over a million likes to the post and the volume was growing steadily. By this time, the news and social media had pieced together all of the articles, YouTube videos, twitter chatter and other accounts about a little brown and white Shih Tzu named Oreo – now widely known as the "Miracle Dog."

It was inevitable that religious leaders would once again take notice of Oreo's fame, or notoriety, depending on the beholder's point of view. It did not matter that no one really claimed or even suggested that the dog, itself, did anything miraculous. The cute creature just seemed to be in the right place at the right time and did what cuddly little creatures, particularly therapy animals, are supposed to do: be consoling and give comfort to those in need. On the other hand, certain officials within the hierarchy of the Church were becoming increasingly worried. The idea that some people – many, actually – were attributing supernatural interventions with religious implications to a mere animal was heretical. It could not be allowed to continue. Then things got worse.

Just before Holy Mass on Thursday morning, Deacon Julio confirmed what Padre Tomas had feared.

"So, it is true then, *los campesinos* are practicing animal idolatry," Padre Tomas said, referring to the common people or peasants in the rural areas outside Delgado."

"Only a few now, but I fear it will spread," Deacon Julio replied. "On my way to visit the sick at the hospital yesterday evening, I counted five little shrines with flowers and a picture of that abominable animal. They all had handwritten petitions or even small signs that seemed to be directed at the dog," the deacon explained.

Perrito bendito
Blessed puppy

Protege mis pollos de los coyotes
Protect my chickens from the coyotes

Oreo consuela a mi hija enferma
Oreo comfort my sick daughter

"Are there any religious symbols associated with what you are calling shrines?" Padre Tomas asked.

"No. None that I can see."

"Have you seen anyone kneel or cross themselves or even hold their hands in a prayful way at those shrines?" the frustrated priest inquired.

"No, Father, I have not."

"Then, all we really have are some piles of rocks with flowers, a few signs or notes that could have been written by anyone and mean anything and a picture of the dog Oreo at each location."

"Yes," Deacon Julio said. "That is for now. But, I can see a cult of idolatry not far off in the future."

"I agree. Immediately after Holy Mass this morning I will call the Archbishop and report this to him. In the meanwhile, please thoroughly address the Church's position on this type of nonsense in your homily Sunday."

As it happened, El Salvador was not the only place where people were beginning to wonder whether the dog Oreo had special gifts – perhaps supernatural gifts. More and more, Oreo's name and deeds arose in a religious context. Some people thought the dog might have been sent from heaven to help lift the sagging spirts of people weighted down by poverty or hopelessness. Others believed that the Almighty was using the dog to intervene directly in the lives of a select few who were in particular need of help. Still others perceived something a little different. They saw an ordinary animal that for some reason was living an extraordinary life of goodness and service to others; a life like that lived by a truly good human being - a saintly one.

Chapter Fifteen

The Archbishop of San Salvador was visibly irritated that Padre Tomas had bothered him with what he termed "ignorant drivel." There were certainly many serious problems currently confronting the archdiocese such as poverty, illiteracy, relationships between the Church and the government and, sadly, scandals within the Church. However, in the archbishop's mind, the possibility that any but the mentally weakest of his flock might be involved in animal idolatry was so remote as to be a non-issue. Nonetheless, he politely thanked Padre Tomas for his telephone call and encouraged him to be watchful in the event there was any substance to the matter in the future. Then, he turned to the Auxiliary Bishop, with whom he was sharing a mid-morning snack of buttery quesadilla pound cake accompanied by El Salvador's signature bourbon bean coffee, and asked, "When is that man scheduled for retirement?"

The auxiliary bishop took a bite of the moist, sweet quesadilla and washed it down with a swallow of the richly flavored coffee. "Another two years, I am afraid. Why do you ask."

The archbishop shared what Padre Tomas had reported concluding with a question. "Have you ever heard of a dog named Oreo?"

"Actually, I have," the auxiliary bishop said. Noting that the archbishop put his cup down and was now looking at him expectantly, he continued. "It is all over the Internet." Then he told his superior about the reports from the United States, including the Reyes incident, which Padre Tomas just mentioned to him. In the end, however, the archbishop concluded that although he had the authority to investigate and decide the merits of supernatural events, none of the reported incidents had occurred in El Salvador. Therefore he could not claim jurisdiction over the matter.

"It looks to me like it is more a problem for the Church in the United States," he concluded. The auxiliary bishop agreed. Grateful that he did not personally have to become involved in the matter, the archbishop took another drink of coffee. Then he offered the auxiliary bishop a second piece of the quesadilla pound cake.

***

According to procedural norms established by the Vatican, the bishop of a diocese in which an alleged supernatural event occurred (such as a miracle or an apparition) has the responsibility and authority to investigate the event and determine its validity. The alleged supernatural events surrounding Oreo occurred in three separate dioceses: Brookfield, Illinois, Cranston, Kansas and Del Rio, Texas. The latter diocese had been recently split off from the San Antonio Archdiocese in order to better meet the needs of a growing southcentral Texas population. It was decided that the best way to apply Vatican procedures in what was now officially referred to as the *Canem Miraculo Inquisitionis*, Latin for Miracle Dog Investigation, was to consolidate the investigation under the supervision of His Excellency, The

Most Reverend Roberto Diaz, Bishop of the Diocese of Del Rio.

"Why me?" Bishop Diaz moaned as he read the letter from His Eminence Cardinal George Broderick, the senior Roman Catholic prelate in the U.S. Southcentral States, who appointed him to head up the *Canem Miraculo Inquisitionis*.

"Because you were outvoted two to one by your peers in the other two dioceses," replied Father Edward Cummings, lead cannon attorney in the Del Rio diocese.

"Well, it is just not fair, Ed," the bishop complained. "This whole matter is foolish enough. How in blazes do you prove or disprove that a mere animal is being used as an instrument of the Lord? Worse yet, how do determine that there is something constructively spiritual about the dog – something supernatural that might not be in direct conflict with Catholic theology? I am going to look like a fool when this is over!"

"No, it's not going to work that way," Father Cummings said. "Your first step is to form a commission of experts to investigate the various incidents and events involving the dog. That will include theologians, canonists like myself, psychologists, doctors and, of course, veterinarians. These experts will help determine the facts, the credibility of witnesses and whether the incidents, themselves are consistent with theological and doctrinal principals."

"Then what?" the bishop asked.

"Then you have three choices. First, you can say that all or at least some of the incidents are true and unexplainable. Alternatively, you can declare that they are not true and that they are easily explainable. Lastly, you can say that you just do not know and cannot make a decision, in which case the issue is shelved for a very long time – decades, perhaps."

"The last two have the greatest appeal to me," the bishop retorted. "I cannot even imagine the consequences of the first one."

"I really think you are making more of this than is warranted," Father Cummings said. "After all, it's not like anyone is thinking about canonizing the creature."

"I wonder," the bishop muttered pensively.

***

With rest stops, it is at least a seven hour drive from Del Rio to Dallas. Bishop Diaz let Father Cummings do most of the driving. The 73 year old prelate had a bad back. He avoided driving long distances because it aggravated his sciatic nerve pain. The two left the bishop's residence right after morning Mass. They stopped in San Angelo for lunch, refueled and planned on arriving at the cardinal's residence in downtown Dallas before the usual end-of-workday traffic delays. Unfortunately, they ran into a detour in Abilene due to an accident and lost an hour, causing them to arrive at the outskirts of Dallas just as traffic was beginning to clog the highways. They pulled into the cardinal's multi-car garage a little after 5:00 pm. It was not possible for them to return to Del Rio that night so they both had been invited to be overnight guests at the cardinal's home.

His Eminence Cardinal Broderick was eager to learn how the bishop and his investigation team planned to go about proceeding with the *Canem Miraculo Inquisitionis*. The cardinal was particularly interested because he was a dog lover. In fact, as Bishop Diaz and Father Cummings were ushered into the cardinal's study, they were welcomed not only by His Eminence, but also by his pride and joy, a little puffy Pomeranian named Wiley. Wiley was a perfectly white Pomeranian, not a trace of yellow or cream in his fur. This was difficult for breeders to achieve because the gene that causes the breed's white coat is recessive.

The three ecclesiastics, bantered over cocktails for a while with small talk before getting to the purpose of the visit. Although according to Vatican protocol, Bishop Diaz could proceed to conduct the *Canem Miraculo Inquisitionis* entirely by virtue of his own authority, it was politically prudent to keep Cardinal Broderick informed about his plans and the status of the investigation. The bishop had now selected the investigation team and was preparing to launch the study. He presented the plan to the cardinal.

"Well, Roberto, I think you did a great job selecting your team," the cardinal said. "My only suggestion is that you consider adding Dr. Emily Frazer at the University of Dallas to your team. Emily holds a Ph.D. in Animal Behavior and Comparative Psychology. She might have an insight into how and why the little critter everyone calls Oreo seems to be able to zero in on people with special needs."

"Thanks George. Good idea. I would appreciate it if you could arrange for her to contact me."

At that moment, the Cardinal's housekeeper Lupita called the trio to the dinner table. Meals at the cardinal's residence were a treat to anticipate: simple, but delicious and well-presented. The fare that night was roast chicken breast over cooked spinach with goat cheese topping and sundried tomatoes preceded by a jumbo shrimp cocktail. Fresh baked cornbread accompanied the entrée, as did a couple bottles of chilled Pinot Grigio di Venezia.

Although they pretended not to take notice, the cardinal's guests caught a glimpse of him occasionally taking a piece of chicken and passing it down to Wiley, who remained obediently at his master's feet during the meal. When dinner was finished, the cardinal suggested that he and his guests take their coffee and dessert in his study so they could continue to discuss the forthcoming *Canem Miraculo Inquisitionis*. As customary after dinner, Wiley left to exit through the pet flap leading out to the residence's backyard that the cardinal had thoughtfully installed on the kitchen door.

A few minutes later and now refreshed, Wiley returned to his master's feet accompanied by Lupita who was carrying another small dog.

"What do you have there, Lupita?" the Cardinal asked.

"Isn't he adorable, Your Eminence?" Lupita replied, as she put the little dog down on the floor. Wiley and the new dog seemed to hit it off well because they were content to circle and sniff each other. "I think he is lost. I have been feeding him and giving him water. Tonight he just walked through Wiley's pet flap as though this was his home."

There was the beginning of a change of mood as the three members of the clergy looked down at the little brown and white dog with floppy ears.

"That's a Shih Tzu, isn't it Your Eminence?" Father Cummings inquired with some concern. The cardinal's earlier smile faded and his only response was a nod. Bishop Diaz clutched the padded arms of his chair tightly.

"Perhaps his owner lives nearby," the cardinal said with caution. "He seems to be perfectly groomed. That suggest to me that his owner takes good care of him."

"Well, he is not just a stray," Lupita declared.

"How do you know that?" Father Cummings asked.

"He has a collar with tags hanging from it," Lupita answered. She bent down and picked the dog up. Then she walked over to Father Cummings and said, "See. One of the tags is a St. Francis medal. That means his owner is likely a Catholic. The other is a name tag." She held the tag up so the priest and the cardinal, both who were now leaning forward in their chairs, could see it clearly. Then, Lupita read what was engraved on the tag, "His name is Oreo," she said smiling.

The Cardinal dropped the coffee cup he had been holding. Father Cummings gasped and the bishop fainted. Oreo squirmed out of Lupita's arms, jumped to the floor and ran toward the kitchen.

"Stop him!" Father Cummings shouted jumping up. "Don't let him get away!"

Lupita began shouting something in Spanish that sounded like a petition to the Virgin for help. She bounded out of the study in pursuit of Oreo, knocking over the coffee and dessert cart. Father Cummings ran after her continuing to shout, "Stop him!" The Cardinal crossed himself and them went to help Bishop Diaz who was struggling to sit up in his chair.

Oreo succeeded in reaching the kitchen where he tore through the pet flap with Wiley following close behind. Unfortunately, by the time Lupita and Father Cummings opened the kitchen door, all they could see in the backyard was Wiley's glistening white coat of fur. Oreo was nowhere to be found.

Chapter Sixteen

The Vatican is an extremely complex and often little understood organization. Completely surrounded by the city of Rome, Vatican City is the smallest independent country in the world. It occupies only 109 acres, which is equivalent to barely one-eighth the size of New York City's Central Park. The Vatican is an absolute monarchy governed by a parliament-like body called the Roman Curia with the pope as its head.

Under the absolute authority of the pope, the Roman Curia consists of two Secretariats and various congregations, councils, tribunals, commissions and offices. The two most important organizations are the Secretariat of State and the Secretariat for the Economy. They are followed by an almost bewildering assortment of subordinate units designed to study, promote and govern all theological, organizational and human related interests and responsibilities of the Catholic Church. One of the lesser known commissions of the Curia is the Pontifical Commission for Supernatural Phenomena, informally known among both clerical and lay persons who deal with it as the Mystic Commission.

The Mystic Commission is comprised of only five permanent members. Heading the commission is Monsignor Enrico Baglio of Argentina, an acquaintance of the current pontiff. The other members are: Dr. Bernard Hudson of Harvard University, an authority on Folklore and Mythology; Reverend Antonio Crespa, a specialist in

Spirituality; Dr. Laura Taglioni of the University of Bologna, specializing in Extraterrestrial Intelligence, and Professor Gerhardt Weber, an astrophysicist at Heidelberg University. Monsignor Baglio, himself, was an exorcist who previously served on the Vatican's congregation for the Clergy. All five of the members of the commission had distinguished careers and are well respected by the Vatican and their peers.

It was hot in the attic of Monsignor Baglio's tiny Chancery office in the Vatican. The monsignor wiped the perspiration from his face with an oversized handkerchief as he thumbed through the six-page report sent to him by Cardinal George Broderick. Monsignor Baglio would have shaken his head in disbelief except that he had long known about the antics of the dog known as Oreo. As an independent city-state, the Vatican ran its own intelligence service; just like it maintained and operated other governmental activities and services usually associated with an independent country including fire, police, security and, as recently as the late 1800s, even a Papal States Army.

The Vatican intelligence service collaborates with the intelligence services of other countries on matters of mutual interest. When an intelligence agency of the United States government picked up cell phone chatter between detained illegal migrants at the Breveton Customs and Border Protection station in Texas and their friends and relatives in several Central American counties about a "Miracle Dog," it took notice. Then, when the chatter clearly began to have a religious connotation, the same service shared a summary of its intercepts with the Vatican. This information was then tied in with earlier reports from Hanford, Illinois, Cranston, Kansas and news media stories about the same subject in general.

Higher, unnamed officials within the Vatican authorized the intelligence profile about the dog to be sent to Monsignor Baglio. In turn, the monsignor convened a special meeting with the members of his commission plus one new temporary, and very reluctant, member whose arrival was scheduled for the following day.

***

Back at the Del Rio residence of Bishop Diaz, Father Edward Cummings stepped into the office of his superior and asked, "Are you feeling any better, Roberto? You looked a little pale at Mass this morning."

"It was a shock. Completely unexpected and completely unexplainable. And right there in the cardinal's residence before all three of us."

"Well, at least it got you off the hook. The Vatican said they intend to pick up the matter, so if you want to shelve it here in the diocese that would be up to you."

"Thanks to the Lord for that!" the bishop responded. "But, you don't look too happy yourself. You should be relieved now that we don't have to worry about the damn dog."

"You don't, but I do," replied a very sour looking Father Cummings.

"What do you mean?" inquired the bishop.

"I'm on my way to the airport," Cummings said. "I got a call from a Monsignor Enrico Baglio who is in charge of the Pontifical Commission for Paranormal Phenomena.

145

I have been appointed to that commission and must be in Rome for a meeting tomorrow. There is an American Airline commuter to Dallas out of here at 2:30 pm. Then, I overnight it to Rome. Baglio told me to expect to be there perhaps a week."

"This is all about the dog?" Diaz asked incredulously.

"I'm afraid so," Cummings replied. "I'm not happy about it, but when the Vatican says come, you go."

"Why in the world do they need a canon lawyer for the commission?"

"I don't know. Baglio is an exorcist. Who knows what they have in mind!" They both laughed.

***

The six of them sat on unpadded wood chairs around an ancient wooden table in a windowless, stuffy room. Father Cummings thought that it was like something right out of the Medieval Inquisition only even more uncomfortable. Monsignor Baglio, who Cummings thought looked old enough to have been born in the Inquisition, gave a perfunctory welcome to the commission's temporary member. He explained that the purpose of the investigation was to determine if there was anything supernatural associated with the known behavior of the dog known as Oreo. He then said, "Remember, the entire proceedings of this commission will be held strictly confidential – *sub pena peccati mortalis*!" his voice rising in tone, emphasizing the "under pain of mortal sin" part. When he finished his opening remarks, he relaxed. "Anybody want an espresso? A little wine, perhaps?"

Two members opted for espresso, one said a Campari and soda would be nice while Cummings and Dr. Laura Taglioni requested a bottle of Pellegrino limonata. Baglio pressed a button under the table. The only door to the room opened and a young, bearded seminarian entered. He went over to the monsignor, who whispered in his ear, and then scurried away. A few minutes later, the seminarian returned pushing a coffee cart loaded with the requested beverages, a plate of biscotti and a dish of antipasto. Father Cummings noted that the seminarian handed the monsignor an insulated cup with his own monogram on it. I would love to know what is in that cup, the canon lawyer wondered.

For the next three days, they recreated all of the known events surrounding the dog named Oreo. They began with his first appearance to Brenda Hopkins at the homeless camp known as "the Heights" in Hanford, Illinois and then continued over 250 miles west to the Cranston Children's Hospital in eastern Kansas. In both of those situations, although the dog's behavior was comforting and motivating, there were only two incidents that were difficult to explain; all the rest were what one might expect from a cuddly little animal that possibly had been trained to be a therapy dog.

The first incident was when Oreo reportedly licked the dachshund Molly that most observers were sure had been hit and killed by a car near Hanford Park. After Oreo licked Molly, the dachshund was reportedly revived and returned to its joyful owner's arms. The commission opined that despite the testimony from a bystander who was an EMT, the dachshund was never examined by a veterinarian and, thus, was never actually certified as

147

having died. Therefore, the commission dismissed that incident.

The second incident was at the Cranston Children's Hospital where an eight-year old boy named Toby Ernst suffering from **acute lymphoblastic leukemia** was in a near terminal condition. According to medical reports, Oreo's unexplained appearance and playful, uplifting behavior with Toby likely help reverse his condition. The commission, however, pointed out that Toby was never diagnosed in an absolute terminal condition and so nothing miraculous actually occurred.

The commission next reviewed Oreo's appearance to Maria Morales Lopez and her son Dacio shortly after the two crossed the Rio Grande River and illegally entered the United States. Not only did Oreo protect Dacio from being attacked by a wild pig, but it also began another series of incidents in which Oreo's playfulness and uplifting behavior helped improve the spirits of the female detainees and children at the Breveton Customs and Border Protection station.

However, the most impressive behavior of Oreo was when his intervention completely defused a life-threatening situation involving a young El Salvadoran boy who was holding a U.S. Congresswoman hostage. Nonetheless, although the commission concluded that it was indeed the dog's calming behavior that precipitated defusing the aforementioned situation, they could not find anything supernatural or paranormal about it. There were, however, other aspects of Oreo's appearances that troubled them greatly and which they could not explain.

"What intrigues me is how the dog got from one location to another," Dr. Hudson stated. "After all, it is over 250 miles from Hanford to Cranston and almost 900 miles from Cranston to Del Rio."

Father Cummings agreed. "Yes. Further, don't forget that he also seemed to travel from Del Rio to the Cardinal's residence in Dallas. That's a distance of over 400 miles."

"Well, there have been cases where a family pet that was lost or stolen somehow found its way back to its owner after traveling many miles," Dr. Taglioni added.

"Yes, but those are rare incidents and in this case there is a consistent pattern where the dog seems to intentionally travel between locations where he is needed," the monsignor pointed out. "That defies understanding."

"How about the fact that wherever he shows up he seems to be perfectly groomed?" The Reverend Crespa asked. "That strongly suggests that his movement from one place to another is a function of either human or spiritual intervention."

"I believe that human intervention is out of the question," Dr. Taglioni stated. "No human could possibly know when and where Oreo's presence was needed. Yet it happened."

"You are a specialist in extraterrestrial intelligence, Dr. Taglioni," the monsignor said. "Are you suggesting that might be a consideration in this case?"

"Well, it has to be a consideration," she said. "It is very unlikely a human was involved in transporting him from one place to another and then making sure he was perfectly groomed for his next assignment."

"It is interesting that you use the word 'assignment' to describe what the dog is doing," Reverend Crespa noted. "Could the dog be on an assignment in a spiritual sense and that he is being used by the Lord to perform good works? What do you think, Monsignor?"

"You all know I am a certified exorcist," Monsignor Baglio said. "I have seen many cases of demonic possession and intervention in human life in my career. I can state that all of the effects of the dog's behavior have been good works – not evil ones."

"So, where does that leave us?" Father Cummings asked.

"I am afraid it leaves us with the possibility that there might be something holy and unexplainable about what the dog is doing," Dr. Hudson said.

"And the problem with that," Father Cummings began, "is that some people are now elevating the dog to the level of a human holy person, which creates quite a problem for the Church."

Chapter Seventeen

The Office of Ethological Research (OER) is a little known subunit of the U.S. Department of Domestic Intelligence, a federal government agency. Part of its shield of obscurity is its name. Not many people outside of the scientific community are aware that ethology is the study of animal behavior, including forms of communication and interaction between animals and between animals and humans. OER is particularly interested in ways that animal interaction with humans might modify human behavior. If a common domestic animal like a dog or cat could be trained to behave in a way that affects human decisions, for example, then its handler might be in a position to manipulate human responses to benefit its particular interest. This would be very disturbing if the handler was a foreign entity working against the security interests of the United States.

Because of this, when news about the unusual antics of the little Shih Tzu named Oreo first came to the attention of the intelligence community, OER took serious notice. Then, intelligence communication intercepts and further news and social media reports showed that public attention to the dog's effect on those with whom it came in contact was beginning to have serious religious implications. The OER interpreted this as a sign that whoever might be handling the animal was being very successful manipulating human behavior. They believed the international ramifications were obvious. OER senior officers decided it was time to act.

Director Justin Jenkins leaned over his desk and with penetrating eyes matching his gaunt frame spoke in almost a whisper to the agents seated in front of him. Agent Jerry Conrad was in his late twenties and had been with the agency for only four years. Lead Agent Martha Burke was thirty-five years old, twice divorced with a teen age daughter and had been with the agency since graduating from college. She was said to be tough as nails, a perfect complement to Jenkin's sour personality.

"I want that dog," Jenkins said grimly. A twenty-five year veteran of OER, Jenkins was in charge of covert ethological operations. From his perspective, everything about this case, code named Canine Retrieval, smelled of foreign intervention. "It's the Russians!" he declared, both hands pressing tightly on his desk. "And, if not them, then the Chinese!"

Despite their personal feelings, neither of the two OER agents dared question Jenkins or, heaven forbid, smile at his fixated demeanor. It was rumored that Jenkins had not smiled in the twenty-five years he had been with OER. The joke behind his back was that he feared a smile would permanently disfigure his face. Considering Jenkin's permanent scowl, some thought anything would be an improvement.

"You have twenty-four hours to give me a plan," Jenkins said. "Find it, bring it here and we will use whatever resources we need to find out first if it is a real animal and then how it was trained and what its mission is." He then slapped his desk signaling that the meeting was over. In unison, both of his subordinates said, "Yes, sir." They rose and left his office with as urgent a look on their face as possible. As they walked down the corridor toward their own offices, however, they gave each other a knowing glance. Agent Conrad muttered under his breath, "Is he out of his mind?" His supervisor, Agent Burke, smiled and said, "I thought he was in good form today."

***

Four thousand four hundred and eighty-one miles from Bethesda, Maryland where the headquarters of OER were located, Monsignor Baglio was leading another meeting of his team discussing the latest international reports about the subject of their *inquisitionis* or investigation, now shortened to the code words *Canem Miraculo,* Miracle Dog.

"There have now been reports that the dog has appeared in every Central American country as well as Chile, Ecuador, Venezuela and Guyana," the monsignor said. "His appearances are always associated with some good work or deed; many of them non-human related. For example, in Ecuador the dog's barking turned back several sheep that were crossing a highway seconds before a speeding truck would have hit them. Then, in Guyana the same type of intervention reportedly saved a mother duck and her ducklings from being swept away when a section of a road collapsed during a flood."

"However, almost none of the reports have been confirmed," Father Cummings noted. "Further, even among the handful that seem to have some validity, there is no evidence that the animal was actually our *Canem Miraculo*."

"It also could be a case of epidemic hysteria," Dr. Taglioni opined. "Someone at an event reports seeing a UFO pass overhead. The next thing you know, almost everyone at the event says they saw it, also."

"Even so," the monsignor said, "the more impressionable indigenous people in some of these areas are beginning to refer to this animal as a holy instrument of the Lord. I received a message from the Bishop of Merida in Venezuela that some members of his diocese are openly praying that the Almighty send the 'little saint' to them to help ease their miseries.

Everyone agreed that was a dangerous turning point. The monsignor continued,

"This morning, my superior, Cardinal Ruffiano, told me that some of the higher ranking members of the Curia are getting nervous. He ordered me to broaden the investigation and said that we should spare no effort to locate the animal and bring it to Rome so that it can be carefully observed and studied."

There was a collective sigh among those around the table. Not possible, they said.

Monsignor Baglio nodded his head in agreement. "Unfortunately, the cardinal said it is our job to determine how this can be done," the monsignor said. "He wants us to prepare a plan and to submit it to him within the next twenty-four hours."

There were gasps of disbelief at the short timeline. "Let's break for an hour," the monsignor suggested.

"When we return I will send out for some pizza and a few cold Peroni's." Then he thought about it and added, "Anyone prefer red wine?"

Five hours, two six packs of Peroni Nastro Azzurro, and two bottles of label less red wine from the cellar of the monsignor's brother Arturo later, the *Canem Miraculo Inquisitionis* team still lacked a plan they felt could be submitted to the cardinal.

"It's all about resources and having any idea where the little Shih Tzu might show up again," Dr. Hudson said. "He might show up anywhere, or nowhere."

"There is one way we could handle this," Father Cummings offered. His comment immediately commanded the attention of everyone seated at the table, now littered with over a dozen empty bottles and six empty Vatican kitchen pizza boxes. "Opus Dei," he calmly said, as though that would be a non-event. There was another collective gasp around the table.

Opus Dei, meaning "Work of God," is a religious organization consisting of lay people, people in religious orders and priests with a membership of over 90,000 men and women in at least 90 countries of the world. The official objective of Opus Dei is to achieve spiritual perfection through personal sacrifice, prayer and corporal mortification, such as taking cold showers, fasting and various forms of physical discomfort even to the extent of pain. The organization has been criticized for its secrecy, which it counters by saying privacy, and for the possibly unorthodox manner in which it conducts its affairs. Globally, Opus Dei was fictionalized in the movies Angels and Demons and The Da Vinci Code.

155

"Opus Dei!" Exclaimed Monsignor Baglio. "You can't be serious."

"I am very serious, Monsignor. You see, I am a member of Opus Dei and I can petition the Prelature for its assistance. Kindly remember that Opus Dei is fully sanctioned by the Church. Yes, with this resource available to us, I believe we can locate and... let's just say temporarily retain our Miracle Dog."

**

Several thousand miles away, Agents Burke and Conrad were not as fortunate. They were stymied by the magnitude of the assignment. But then, Agent Burke had an idea.

"This is an international problem, isn't it Director?" she asked.

"Yes, of course," Jenkins responded. "Why do you ask?"

"Well, considering the fact that our agency lacks the resources to accomplish our mission, why not get Interpol involved?" Agent Burke asked, referring to the internationally acclaimed law enforcement agency.

Director Jenkins looked up from his desk at the woman and tried to smile, but the pain was too much. "That's one of the attributes I like about you, Agent Burke, resourcefulness." Unfortunately, Jenkins was not aware that Agent Burke also had a vulnerability. She loved dogs. In fact, she had two female Yorkies she privately referred to as her "girls."

Chapter Eighteen

The infamous Italian crime syndicate Camorra controls most of the racketeering, money laundering, prostitution, drug trafficking and related criminal activities in the region of Campania and its principal city Naples. A lesser known, but cruel and insidious enterprise of Camorra, is its control of most of Campania's *Canili Refugi* or public dog kennels. Tragically, Italy is overrun by stray dogs – over 600,000 of them. Only one-third of these animals have been caught and are in kennels or shelters. The problem is that the mob, including Camorra, the Mafia and other Italian criminal enterprises, controls most of those shelters.

There are many reasons why there are so many stray dogs in Italy. Sadly, every year about 135,000 cats and dogs are abandoned by their owners, many simply dumped along a highway or a city street. Thousands of these animals are left to roam, struggling to find food and water wherever they can. Thousands of others are captured by the various municipalities and incarcerated in the *Canili*. Keeping dogs imprisoned in the *Canili* is a lucrative business in Italy. The European Union funds the *Canili* by paying them €8.50 per animal per day. That is a lot of money. No wonder the Camorra and other mobs have taken control of so many *Canili* throughout the country, especially in the southern regions.

One of the more notorious and cruel shelters is the *Canili in Collina*, Kennels in the Hills, located outside the town of Caserta, about an hour north of Naples on the highway toward Rome. Because the more dogs a *Canili* has, the more money from the government its owners make, the *Canili in Collina* houses from two to three hundred dogs at any time. The more the better. Unfortunately, almost all of the animals, except for the breeds that would command more money by their sale, are treated inhumanely. They are given the minimum food and water to keep them alive and little else. In time, the dogs die from malnutrition, disease and simply because the broken animals have given up the will to live. Euthanasia of even ill dogs is unlawful in Italy; so, the owners of mob shelters simply let the animals suffer until they die and then quickly replace them with others.

One day, three weeks after the urgent meetings held by OER and the *Canem Miraculo* teams, a little brown and white Shih Tzu was found wandering the streets of Caserta. It was taken by one of the Caserta residents to the *Canili in Collina* where the manager immediately determined he could sell the dog for much more than the €10 he paid the Caserta resident. Full blooded Shih Tzu's could command €400 or more. Next, the manager made what later turned out to be a mistake. He took a photo of the dog and posted it on the Internet advertising it for sale. It was a cute photo that also happened to clearly show the metal tag hanging from the dog's collar with the name Oreo engraved on it.

It was Timothy, the seminarian who also serves as one of Monsignor Baglio's assistants, who first saw the Internet post advertising Oreo for sale. The minute he saw it, he downloaded the photo and rushed to show it to the monsignor.

"My God, we have found him!" the monsignor exclaimed. He immediately contacted the rest of the team who all rushed over to the monsignor's office in the Vatican Chancery Building. Once seated around the table in the tiny conference room, their next step was to decide how to obtain the dog.

"I cannot believe he is here in Italy," Reverend Crespa said. But, since he is only three hours south of here, why don't we simply go down there and buy him?"

Doctors Hudson and Taglioni agreed, while the others were unsure. Father Cummings suggested caution.

"This must be a covert operations," he said. "No matter how we might handle the purchase, there would be too many questions asked and the purchase could possibly be traced to us."

"I agree," Professor Weber said. "There has to be another way we can get hold of the dog."

"Well Father Cummings, you said you are a member of Opus Dei, surely they could help us acquire the animal."

"Yes, of course. I'll take care of it," the canon lawyer said.

On the other side of the Atlantic Ocean, Agent Jerry Conrad rushed into the office of Agent Martha Burke waving a communication intelligence intercept he had just received.

"They found the dog!" he shouted. "The damn thing is in some type of animal shelter in, of all places, Italy."

Agent Burke picked up the phone on her desk and buzzed her boss, Director Jenkins. "I saw the same report," Jenkins said. "I want you and Conrad on a plane to Italy immediately. Fly into NAS Naples, get a car and pick him up. Covertly, of course," he stressed. Jenkins was referring to the U.S. Naval Support Activity station adjacent to the Naples, airport in Capodichino, Italy.

An hour and a half later, Agents Burke and Conrad were aboard a Gulfstream C-37A speeding across the Atlantic toward their destination over four thousand miles away. Burke was frantically using the aircraft's secure communication system to make arrangements they would need upon arrival, including special tools, night vision equipment and clothing. She also ordered a large cage in which the dog would be placed for their return flight to Joint Base Andrews. When she was done with the essential work, she texted her daughter, telling her she would be gone for a few days and to be sure to give the "girls" a special hug and extra treats.

***

Lucio Mangano was the proprietor of an art shop in Salerno, Italy that sells reproductions of ancient Pompeiian and Herculaneum art. He was also a very devout Catholic and a faithful member of Opus Dei, holding a type of membership called Supernumerary. Lucio lived a traditional life. He had a wife and children and together they believed that God should be a part of their daily life. Lucio was also a master thief. Before his marriage to Luisa and his conversion to a reborn spiritual life, he had served five years in Rome's famous Regina Coeli (Queen of Heaven) prison for art theft. But, now Lucio was reformed – at least in a manner of speaking.

Over the centuries, an incredible amount of priceless artwork has been stolen from Catholic churches throughout Europe; much of this during the past centuries when invading armies tore through Europe and plundered whatever riches they could find. During the past century, the Vatican has had a program of recovering as much of the lost artwork as possible. Often, the Vatican recovered its rightfully owned art objects by legal means, such as through court action or through the auspices of the United Nations. Sometimes, however, those efforts were not enough. That is where Lucio and Opus Dei entered the scene. Once Opus Dei located stolen objects belonging to the Church, it notified the Vatican which usually authorized it to recover the same. Lucio was one of the covert operators who assisted in that effort.

"You cannot possibly be serious!" Lucio said to his contact, an Opus Dei Numerary known to him only as Mario. "I am a skilled professional. In my career, I have helped Opus Dei recover hundreds of stolen chalices, candelabras, statues and manuscripts. I was even part of the team that just this past year recovered the 16th Century Statue of Michael the Archangel, Patron Saint of Monteroduni. Now you want me to steal a lowly dog? You're crazy! I won't do it." Momentarily, Lucio forgot that obedience is one of the virtues drilled into an Opus Dei supernumerary.

It was cloudy all of the next day, which meant that the night would be quite dark – perfect for Lucio's purpose. He told his wife that he had to attend to Church business, an euphemism meaning that he was off on another covert Opus Dei mission. Then, he loaded all the clothing and equipment he thought he would need into his black 2013 Fiat 500 and set out on the nearly two hour drive to *Canili in Collina* via routes E841 and then A30.

Earlier that evening, Agents Burke and Conrad arrived at NAS Naples. During the flight, Agent Burke read intelligence reports about the stray dog problem in Italy and the shocking conditions in which these poor animals were made to live – if one could even call such inhumane treatment "living." She was especially horrified when she read about the shelter where Oreo was located, *Canili in Collina*. It was one of the worst in all of the region of Campania. The intelligence report described the shelter in considerable detail including the fact that the shelter's human keepers left it unguarded from 10:00 pm until 6:00 am every day. The two agents got in a black Fiat 500 OER obtained for them and headed off toward Caserta and the animal shelter a few miles beyond the city.

Shortly after passing Caserta, Lucio pulled into an Autogrill rest stop where he ordered a double espresso and a piece of ricotta cheesecake. He thought the extra caffeine would be helpful later that night. However, he also had a sweet tooth and always had a little *dolce*, dessert, about that time of night. While he was enjoying his late night snack, he noticed two tourists come into the Autogrill and order cappuccinos to go. The minute he heard them order cappuccinos he knew they were American. No Italian or, for that matter, European would drink a cappuccino at any time of day except morning. He noticed their black leather clothing and assumed they were motorcyclists. Then he realized he was wearing much the same type of outfit. Curious, he thought.

Agent Conrad was momentarily confused when the lock on the Fiat he was trying to enter did not open as he pressed the remote key. Both he and Agent Burke smiled when they realized they were trying to enter a similar Fiat parked just a couple of spaces from their vehicle. Fifteen minutes later, Agent Conrad pulled off the highway onto an unmarked dirt road that led up a gently rising hill. It was very dark and the twisting road was completely deserted. The two consulted their GPS and concluded they were less than a half kilometer from *Canili in Collina*. They spotted a rutted weed overgrown farm road on the left and decided to pull a little off the dirt road, leave the car there and walk the rest of the way. Prudently, Agent Conrad turned the car around facing the way they had come to facilitate a rapid exit if necessary. Then they got out of the car, donned a backpack each and stealthily proceeded up the road.

After enjoying the last of the cheesecake and espresso, Lucio felt refreshed and alert. He got back in his car and drove the remaining distance to an unmarked dirt road that his GPS indicated would take him to *Canili in Collina* only two kilometers further. When he was about half a kilometer from the shelter, he spotted what seemed to be an abandoned rutted and weed overgrown farm road on his right. He pulled the car a little way up the road, turned it around in case he needed to make a hasty exit and got out of the car. Then he donned a backpack and began stealthily walking up the road.

Canili in Collina was laid out in the shape of a square, about one hundred feet on each side. The building was surrounded by a six foot wall and had only one entrance, a vehicle gate that was left open during the hours the shelter was operating but that was locked at night. The two OER agents had decided to make this a quick snatch. They did not want to leave evidence that anyone had been in the shelter that night; so, instead of breaking open the vehicle gate, they simply and easily climbed over the fairly low wall. The minute their feet touched the ground they faced an appalling sight: dozens of large cages crammed with the most pathetic looking dogs one could imagine. They were also met with the loudest uproar of barking and dog wails they had ever heard.

They shined their military issued LED penlights around, taking in the terrible scene. Agent Burke was completely stricken with disgust. There must have been two or three hundred dogs cramped so tightly into cages that they many could not even turn around. She wondered how anyone could treat these beautiful creatures so callously. However, she was tough and no matter how heartrending the scene, she had a job to do. They went from cage to cage until at one, a little brown and white dog with floppy ears sauntered to where they were standing and sat down, like it was evaluating them.

"That's him!" Agent Burke exclaimed in a hushed voice.

"Yep, I can see the collar with the two tags hanging from it and the name Oreo on one of them," Agent Conrad said focusing his penlight on the dog.

Agent Burke reached into her backpack and took out a special harness that would fit over and secure the dog so he could not escape. There was no lock on the cage door so all they had to do was open it, retrieve Oreo and be on their way. Rather than resist, Oreo leaped into Agent Burke's arms and began licking her face. She could not resist the adorable creature and cradled him in her arms before coming to her senses.

"We have to go," she said over the howling and wailing of the other dogs. But then, as she looked around at the misery around her she thought about her little two Yorkies at home, Trish and Cloe, her two girls. She thought about the comfort, love and security they had compared with the inhumane conditions these dogs had to endure. The more she thought about it, the more angry she got. Angry and sad – very sad. Tears formed in her eyes and then she began to cry. She sat down on the ground cuddling Oreo and began wailing almost as loud as the chorus of dogs around her. Agent Conrad was stunned. However, he, too, was appalled at the egregiously abusive conditions he saw these animals were kept in.

Finally, Agent Burke stood up and said. "I am sorry, Jerry. I will likely get fired for this, but I will not simply leave all of these dogs here to suffer and die a terrible death. She put Oreo down and began going around opening the doors of the cages. As she did, dozens and then scores of dogs streamed from the cages and flooded the center part of the shelter. Agent Conrad could not take it anymore, himself, and began helping her opening the cages.

"What are we going to do with them?" he asked.

"We are going to open that damn vehicle gate and let them loose," she said. "I don't know what is going to happen to them out there, but at least they have a chance to survive. They don't have any chance in this horrid place."

Lucio heard the noise of barking, howling and animal wailing when he was still some distance from the shelter. He could not imagine what was causing the dogs to behave that way unless, perhaps, a wolf had gotten into the shelter grounds. Yes, that must be it, he thought. A wolf. He must be extra careful. His plan was to pick the lock on the vehicle gate, enter the shelter and make a quick snatch of the dog Oreo. He took out a net bag from his backpack into which he intended to place the animal after he caught it.

Inside the shelter, Agents Burke and Conrad finished opening the last of the cages. They were surrounded by barking and howling dogs, many jumping on them as if ecstatic that they were being set free. Oreo was now standing near the vehicle gate as though anticipating that something more was about to happen.

"Let's get out of here!" Agent Conrad said. Both he and Agent Burke ran toward the vehicle gate, unlocked it from the inside and threw the gate open. At that very instant, Lucio had walked up to the gate, taken out his prized twelve-piece pick set and was preparing to make quick work of the lock. Instead, the double doors of the gate were suddenly thrown open and nearly three hundred dogs, led by a little brown and white Shih Tzu, rushed out trampling him in the process.

Agents Burke and Conrad followed the dogs as they spread out into the countryside running toward their freedom. They practically stumbled over Lucio, who was staggering to stand up and brush himself off. Lucio looked at the two agents and said, *"Voi chi siete*, who are you?" Then he recognized them from the Autogrill. *"Ah, gli americani."*

Agents Burke and Conrad looked at each other and then took off running down the hill toward their car. Lucio ran, also. Not chasing them, but rather because he feared all the noise would rouse someone's attention and he would be caught.

They reached their cars the same time. Lights out, both black Fiats spun their wheels on the gavel of the farm road they were on and sped to make their getaway. Unfortunately, the side farm roads they left their cars on were opposite each other. Both cars reached the main dirt road at the same time and...well, you know what happened next.

***

The two OER agents and the Opus Dei Supernumerary sat together at a table in the all night Autogrill. A bottle of red wine and a plate of *salume* and *formaggio* rested on the table in front of them. Both parties had already made contact with their respective superiors. The mission failed, they said. The problem was that their car was involved in an accident and that they were unable to reach *Canili in Collina* as planned. Lucio's boss Mario was furious, but not half as angry as OER Director Jenkins. Although Lucio did not speak English and neither Agent Burke nor Agent Conrad spoke Italian, they were able to use a Google Voice Translate app on their cell phones to communicate with each other and concoct the cover story – a partially true story if you discounted the timeline.

Both cars were damaged in the collision. However, the cars were sufficiently drivable so that they could reach the Autogrill parking lot. Agent Conrad was the one who had the idea about using Google Translate to break the communication barrier.

"What a mess?" Lucio said via his translator.

"At least none of us are hurt," Agent Burke said on hers.

"Now what?" Agent Conrad asked via his.

"If we call the *carabiniere* there will be many questions – to many, I am afraid," Lucio said.

"You mean the Italian federal police like our State Police," Agent Conrad said.

Lucio nodded. "Something like that," he said despondently.

"Well then," Agent Burke said. "Let's have a little more of that delicious soppressata and gorgonzola and then hope our cars can make it back to wherever we came from."

Lucio refilled their glasses with the last of the red wine. As they lifted the glasses in salute, Agent Burke said, "To Oreo and all his friends. May he lead them to a happy life!"

Chapter Nineteen

Monsignor Baglio's elbows were on the table in front of him. His hands held his bowed head as he groaned, "He was right in our grasp and he got away! How could such a thing happen?"

"The Opus Dei operative claims his car was hit by another car that was speeding away from the shelter," Professor Weber said. "Should we believe him?"

"What does it matter?" Father Cummings asked. "The fact is that we lost a good chance to get the dog. I will tell you that according to my contacts something very strange happened at *Canili in Collina* last night. They claim that somehow all of the dogs held in that horrible place got loose – that would obviously include Oreo."

"I heard that someone at the Autogrill north of Caserta spotted two damaged black Fiats in the parking lot and called the *carabiniere*. However, by the time they arrived those two cars were gone," Reverend Crespa said.

"Yes, there is a strong rumor that more than one party was trying to capture the dog the same night," Father Cummings said. "What an incredible mess!"

Monsignor Baglio sat back in his chair, raised his twenty ounce insulated Yeti cup to his lips and drank heavily from it.

"That's not Pellegrino mineral water is it?" Dr. Hudson inquired.

"No," the monsignor said candidly. Before anyone could question him further, he pressed the button attached to the underside of the table. Timothy, the seminarian appeared immediately through the meeting room door. The monsignor nodded to him and a moment later, the seminarian rolled in a cart holding an ice bucket, five glasses and a liter bottle of Johnnie Walker Gold Label Reserve Scotch. He glanced around the table and then began filling glasses as each of the men nodded their approval. Finally, the lone female member of the team, Dr. Laura Taglioni, nodded saying, "What the hell, why not."

***

St. Francis of Assisi was a complex man who exchanged a life of wealth and even debauchery for extreme poverty. He eventually became a preacher, an ordained deacon and he founded what today is known as the Order of St. Francis – the Franciscans. He also loved nature and considered all living creatures his brothers and sisters as much as his human family. That is why he became the patron saint of ecologists and animals.

The *Cammino di Francesco* or Way of St. Francis, is a meandering trail of ancient Roman roads between Florence, Italy and Rome that traces a route often traveled by St. Francis of Assisi. Today, most of those ancient Roman roads have been turned into trails and paths used by hikers, bikers and nature lovers. Along the route, located between the walled cities of Assisi and Spoleto, lies Trevi, a beautiful Umbrian town on the top of a hill that overlooks the wide plain of the Clitunno River system.

Trevi traces its origin to the First Century B.C. The Roman author and naturalist Pliny the Elder once identified the town as home to the ancient Umbrians. In medieval times, St. Francis is known to have passed through Trevi on several occasions preaching and doing works of charity. Today, hikers frequenting the *Cammino di Francesco* often stop in Trevi where they visit religious and historical sites within the city including the *Santuario* of the *Madonna delle Lacrime*, the Church of Our Lady of Tears, known for its beautiful votive works of art including a section dedicated to St. Francis.

Bill and Claudia Harris took off their backpacks and sat on a low stone wall, probably a property marker, about one mile outside the pedestrian gate leading into the walled city of Trevi, now home to about 4,000 people. They both looked up at the city perched high on the hill above them and wondered why anyone would want to live in such a steep, crowded place with incredibly narrow alleys and streets. Entrance and egress from the city was limited. A lone single-vehicle road passed through a stone gate and circled up and around to the top of the walled city and was available to only to authorized commercial and emergency traffic. Most other vehicles had to park outside of the city walls in a large *parcheggio* or parking lot.

"Well, are you up to climbing the streets of another walled city on a hill?" Bill asked his young wife. The intrepid pair had begun their trek at Assisi and were working their way down the *Cammino di Francesco* to Spoleto. They visited all of the small cities and towns along the route overnighting at an *agriturismo* or country inn much like a hostel. Trevi was about thirty-five kilometers north of Spoleto, their destination. It was already after noon and, because of the difficult terrain *Cammino di Francesco* passed through, there was no way they could hike the remaining distance to Spoleto that day.

"We'll never make Spoleto tonight," Claudia said. "So, we might want to either stay at a hostel in Trevi or in an agriturismo outside the city. Personally, I prefer the latter – we have had better food and accommodations at the farm facilities than in the hot towns."

"OK, but do you want to see the city?"

"I don't know. How many medieval streets, buildings, churches, piazzas and quaint fountains can the mind absorb. I mean, they are all wonderful, but I am getting a case of "medieval overload," Claudia declared.

"Yeah," Bill agreed. "I know what you mean." He held up a guidebook and said, "Look, here is my suggestion. That bell tower you can see a little down the road is the *Santuario* of the *Madonna delle Lacrime*. The guide book says it has some beautiful artwork inside including what they call votive artwork in the St. Francis section."

"What is votive artwork?" Claudia asked.

"The guidebook says it is usually folk art showing scenes about some miraculous event in which a saint or holy person intervened with God to heal a serious illness or grant a special favor."

"Well, that's different," Claudia said. "We haven't seen anything like that yet."

"Right," Bill replied. "So, let's amble over to that church, see what there is to see and then look for a place to stay for the night."

"Sounds good to me," Claudia said. "But, right after that I want to find an *enoteca* where we can get a glass of wine and a plate of antipasto!"

The Santuario was built in the early Fifteenth Century in the Renaissance style popular at that time. The interior is laid out in the shape of a single nave Latin cross. Numerous small chapels dot the interior of the church including the larger Chapel of St. Francis that contains a painting titled The Deposition of Christ by the famous painter Lo Spagna. Small panels of various scenes adorn the base of the walls in the chapels surrounding the interior of the church including several votive scenes depicting folk art of the times.

Bill and Claudia took their time enjoying the priceless artwork throughout the Santuario. They saved the Chapel of St. Francis for last. When they reached that chapel, they noticed an older priest accompanied by two younger men, seminarians, they presumed, standing at one of the panels. A camera on a tripod had been set up and soft studio portrait lighting was shining on the panel.

"I wonder why they are photographing that particular panel," Claudia asked her husband.

"I have no idea," Bill said. "If you'd like, I'll ask that guy who seems to be a priest. How do you go about addressing a Catholic priest?" he wondered aloud. "Reverend?"

A male voice from behind them said, "Father would usually be the correct title. However, in this case the fuchsia piping on the cassock he is wearing indicates he is a monsignor." Then the man quickly added, "I'm sorry. I could not help overhearing your question."

They turned around to see a bespectacled middle age man in clerical garb standing behind them. "I am Father Ed Cummings from the Diocese of Del Rio in Texas," he said. "I have a feeling that you two are not from the U.S."

"Canada, actually," Bill said. "Toronto. I am Bill Harris and this is my wife Claudia. How did you guess that we are not from the U.S.?"

"Well, it's true that over the past few decades there has been a great leveling of accent between our two countries. However, when I hear someone pronounce 'about' as 'aboot,' it is a clear giveaway." All three laughed at the priest's keen observation.

"Are all of the panels being photographed for some reason?" Claudia asked.

"No, in fact they have to be quick about photographing this one. They had to get special permission for this shoot from the Vatican's Commission on Antiquities because bright artificial lighting can damage the pigment in old paintings and the one you are looking at is over four hundred years old."

"What is so special about that one?" Bill inquired.

"Let me show you," Father Cummings said as he led the pair closer to the panel that was a square measuring one meter on each side. Within the panel, the painting depicted a pastoral scene showing St. Francis surrounded by animals. A flock of birds sat attentively on the branches of a tree while St. Francis, wood staff in his right hand, seemed to be preaching to them. On the ground were several domestic animals including a lamb, a calf, a few rabbits and squirrels and two or three cats and dogs. A little dog was tugging at the bottom of the saint's brown robe trying to call his attention to a baby deer who seemed to have fallen into the stream behind him and was frantically struggling to get out of the water.

"That is an interesting scene," Claudia said. "However, what is special about it?"

"Take a close look at the dog," Father Cummings said. "Describe it to me."

"Well, it is brown and white. Fairly small – maybe twelve or fifteen pounds, I would suspect," Bill said.

"He is really cute," Claudia said. "I mean you can clearly see it is a male. Also, he has floppy ears."

"What kind of breed would you say it is," Father Cummings asked.

"Umm, maybe a Pomeranian or a Lhasa Apso," Claudia proposed.

"If you take a good look at the dog's face, you can see that it is flat like a pug. That means the dog is brachycephalic or that its breed has an elongated soft palate," the priest explained. "The only dog that fits everything you described is a Shih Tzu, a dog bred by the ancient Chinese to be both an excellent companion and a good watch dog."

175

"OK, but why are they bothering to take a photograph of a Shih Tzu with St. Francis?" Bill wondered.

Father Cummings reached into the leather portfolio he was carrying and pulled out a photograph downloaded from the Internet. "Have you ever seen this photo?" he asked, knowing that anyone in the western hemisphere who watches TV or follows the social media on the Internet would have likely seen it.

Claudia gasped and grabbed Bill's arm. "Oh my God, Bill. It's that dog. The one they call the Miracle Dog."

"Yeah," Bill said. "It sure looks like him but how does that fit in with this painting?"

"That is what we are trying to find out," Father Cummings said. "We have a theory and we are trying to…"

He was interrupted by a deep, low sound followed by a feeling that someone was gently shaking the floor of the church. Claudia grabbed Bill more tightly. Then they noticed that the chandeliers hanging from the ceiling of the church were swaying slightly.

"That was a tremor!" Father Cummings said as everyone in the church looked up at the ceiling. "I think we would be safer outside!" Everyone exited the Santuario as fast as they could and gathered in the *piazza* outside where they stood in a group assessing the situation. Father Cummings introduced Bill and Claudia to Monsignor Baglio and soon the young Canadian couple learned how the Church was dealing with the matter concerning a certain Shih Tzu named Oreo.

Chapter Twenty

The Central Headquarters for Italy's Istituto Nazionale di Geofisica e Vulcanologia (INGV), the National Institute for Geophysics and Volcanology, is located in a large, semi-circular, glass-faced building nestled between two roads, Via Vigna Murata and Via Luca Gaurico, eight kilometers south of the center of Rome. Among its responsibilities, INGV is tasked with monitoring seismic activity throughout the country. Two tectonic fault lines pass through Italy. The North-South fault line runs down the Apennines while the East-West fault line runs from Naples westward. Because of the active geophysical nature of Italy's topography, numerous detection devices have been placed along these fault lines by INGV to monitor seismic and volcanic activity.

Dr. Lorenzo Bernardi, a geophysicist at INGV, stood next to his assistant, Andrea Russo, as they watched the pattern of seismic waves being recorded on the computerized seismograph in front of them display the pattern of a typical foreshock.

"Where is the epicenter of this one?" Bernardi asked.

"Four miles north of Trevi at a depth of ten kilometers," Russo promptly responded.

"They are so damned difficult to predict," Bernardi said. "You would think that by this time we would have mastered the science, or art, of earthquake prediction. But, there are so many variables involved in analyzing plate tectonic stresses that it is clear we are still a long way off in pinpointing when an earthquake will occur."

"Uh huh," Russo agreed. "This one registered only 2.7 on the Richter Scale. It was barely felt. But, combined with the data from the array of detection stations running down the Apennines, it strongly suggests that there is more to follow - likely a much larger one. "

"Yeah, most likely," Bernardi agreed. "Well, I think we should put out a warning that an earthquake of light to moderate intensity might occur in the central Apennines within the next twenty-four to forty-eight hours. Hopefully, people in that region will pay attention and take the proper precautions."

Russo grunted. "I'll get right on it. But, from a practical perspective, what are they going to do? Sleep out in the streets tonight?"

Bernardi shrugged his shoulders. He walked away from the computer that was still recording seismic activity and returned to his office. A half hour later, notices were sent out from INGV to fire, police and public works offices and to hospitals and all other first responders throughout Umbria that an earthquake of magnitude 3.0 to 5.0 might occur in the region within the next twenty-four to forty-eight hours. The same warning was also communicated to the public via that day's radio and TV weather broadcasts. As usual in seismically active Italy, such warnings were fairly common and thus were mostly ignored.

***

The small but beautiful walled city of Trevi, Italy lies in the province of Perugia in the region of Umbria. Much of the construction within the city took place during the medieval period between the eleventh and fifteenth centuries. Construction of buildings in that period followed the traditional Roman style in which stone and mortar outer walls were joined by wood beams that supported the various number of floors or stories. The floors were connected by brick or wood stairways, often on the exterior of the building or through semi-enclosed passageways. In most cases the number of stories was limited to four. One of the reasons for this was technical; the taller the building the wider the required base. The other reason was more practical; climbing even four stories carrying supplies and children was a chore.

Stella Righi, her husband, Giorgio and their eighteen-month old baby daughter Anna lived in a rented 700 square foot, one-bedroom, one-bath apartment on Via Della Campana in one of the older parts of the city. Giorgio was a corporal in the Italian Army attached to the 9th Parachute Assault Regiment. Currently, he was stationed in Afghanistan as part of a small United Nations Contingent. So, Stella had to fend for herself until Giorgio completed his tour and returned home in three more months. Meanwhile, an elderly lady next door to Stella took care of baby Anna when Stella was working at the Trevi Police Office on Piazza Mazzini where she was employed as a clerk.

Typical of many Italian walled cities where space was limited, only residents could park within the city, itself. Tourists and other visitors – except drivers of supply and service vehicles – were required to park outside the city gates and walk into the city from that location. As a resident of the city, Stella was permitted to use a parking lot on Via Lucarini a few blocks from her home. However, this meant that she had to walk through several tight alleys and twisting passageways over uneven paving stones every time she needed to use her car, go shopping or go to work. Then, she had to climb several sets of stairs to reach her fourth floor apartment. It was all very tiring.

Following her after-work routine, Stella first fed Anna then made herself a little risotto with parmesan cheese and broccoli. After dinner, she bathed Anna and put her to bed in the crib crammed between the double bed she and Giorgio used and the armoire holding most of their wardrobe. Next, she booted up her computer and spent a few facetime minutes chatting with Giorgio, who she missed dearly. She could hardly wait for the next three months to pass so they could be together again. Before retiring for the night, herself, Stella laid out the clothes she and Anna would need the next day. Then, she took a quick shower and went to bed. It was 11:15 pm.

There was no warning. The 6.3 magnitude earthquake struck Trevi and the surrounding towns in the province of Perugia at 5:17 am when most of the walled city's residents were still sleeping. The sun had not yet risen over the horizon, so Trevi was still enveloped by the darkness of the night. As soon as the tremor hit, those who could began streaming out of their houses and apartments into the narrow streets and alleys. Cracks appeared on the facades of several buildings and an ancient tower collapsed. A number of people standing in the streets were injured by debris falling on them from buildings on either side of the streets. There did not seem to be any major damage – except to the collapsed tower and an old apartment building on Via Della Campana – the building in which Stella and her baby lived.

As soon as the tremor hit, an alarm was sounded throughout the walled city. Trevi's emergency services including first responders, firefighters and police immediately gathered at the town square called Piazza Mazzini. Volunteers from the surrounding area rushed to help the injured and to assist emergency personnel as needed. In a small city where everyone knew everyone else, there was no shortage of help. But, they were not prepared for what they saw on Via Della Campana. One of the oldest buildings in the city had been split in half by the earthquake with one half completely collapsing into rubble on the street. The other half looked like a child's dollhouse with the remaining rooms completely exposed. Further, the remaining half of the building was tilted at a dangerous angle. Rescuers were blocked from access to the interior of the building by a portion of the brick and stone stairway that had also collapsed.

As the first light of dawn began to cast its weak light on the horrific scene, one of the police officers shouted, "That's Stella Righi's apartment!" Meanwhile, both emergency personnel and volunteers were combing through the rubble searching for anyone trapped in the debris of the collapsed part of the building. Here and there a cry was heard and rescuers rushed over to render what assistance they could. One of them shouted, "Over here. Quickly! It's Mrs. Alfonsi." Mrs. Alfonsi was the elderly woman who cared for Stella's baby Anna while Stella was working at the police office.

"Has anyone seen Stella and the baby?" someone called out. Just then, another part of the building collapsed and the rescuers below scurried to safety. The lone firetruck owned by the city made its way up Via Della Campana cautiously and stopped as close as it could to the collapsed building. Firefighters leaped out of the vehicle and began extending the ladder so they could examine the exposed parts of the building's apartments. They made a visual inspection of each exposed section and were able to reach two badly injured residents on the lower floors. They feared, however, that others might be buried under the rubble below. When the aerial ladder was extended to Stella's apartment, the firefighter standing at the top shouted, "I see Stella! She is right here at the edge of the floor. I think she is unconscious."

His partner, who was managing the controls of the ladder, inched it closer to the exposed edge of the building that was now sloping sharply downward. The firefighter on the ladder stretched and dragged the inert body of Stella closer to the ladder and with all the strength he could muster latched on to her. "She is alive!" he exclaimed as he passed her to another firefighter who was standing behind him on the ladder.

"How about the baby?" one of the firefighters on the ground shouted. The firefighter who had just rescued Stella simply shook his head. "I'm going to try to get on the floor so I can look for her," he said. But then, an aftershock was felt and the remaining part of the building shuddered.

"Back, back!" The fire chief supervising the operation commanded. And the operator of the ladder swung it out of danger as another part of the building's exterior collapsed.

There was nothing they could do. Workers were trying to clear the blocked stairway, but there was still no space large enough for a person to crawl through. The rest of the building seemed as if it would collapse at any moment. The fire chief decided he could not allow his men to risk their lives further. Besides, it was almost certain that, tragically, Stella's baby had already perished in the initial collapse.

As the fire chief wiped his brow and shielded the tears in his eyes, he heard a furious bark and felt something tugging at boots. He looked down and saw a small brown and white dog frantically trying to get his attention. The dog tugged hard at his boots and then ran a few feet toward the collapsed stairs. When that did not get a response, the dog repeated the process.

"What the hell is that dog doing?" the fire chief asked. But, then the dog ran toward the rubble on the stairs, climbed over some of the debris and disappeared into what appeared to be a hole in the fallen bricks. "That's the strangest damn thing," the fire chief said.

A few moments later, the wailing of a small child could be heard somewhere up in the remaining part of the apartment building. Everyone looked up and began shouting. "Quiet!" the fire chief commanded. "Where is the crying coming from?"

"There!" somebody said pointing to the exposed portion of the uppermost apartment. There was a gasp, accompanied by many shouts, "My God! It's Stella's baby," a police officer shouted in horror as everyone below saw a toddler crawl toward the edge of the torn floor. "Oh dear Lord," another said. "She'll fall and be killed!"

But, before the child could reach the end of the torn floor, the dog that had been tugging at the fire chief's boot rushed forward and placed himself between the child and the edge of the building. The dog barked and the child stopped moving forward.

"Get that ladder back up there immediately," shouted the fire chief. His command was unnecessary because the ladder was already on its way up and two firefighters, one behind the other, were climbing it as fast as they could.

"I can't reach her!" shouted the first firefighter. Move the ladder closer!"

"Careful, the weight of the ladder might collapse the building," someone on the ground warned.

They moved the ladder within inches of the floor of Stella's exposed bedroom. As they inched the ladder closer to the edge, the dog move away from little Anna and sat behind her, giving the firefighter a better chance to reach her. Still, she was a few inches away from his grasp. Then, the dog stood up and barked at the child, startling her. Instinctively, she moved away from the dog into the waiting hands of the firefighter who was stretched as far as he could. He grabbed her and pulled her securely to him to the joyful shouts and applause of everyone below, many who were filming the entire event.

However, the extra weight of the child in the firefighters' arms forced the overextended ladder down enough that it pressed against the floor. A loud crack was heard and the floor trembled. Once again, the fire chief ordered, "Back, back!" as the ladder swung away from the building. The little dog, that was clearly one of the heroes of the rescue, slid to the edge of the floor as the remainder of the building began to crumble. At the last instant, the dog leaped away from the building, but flailed in the air disappearing into the cloud of dust rising from the rubble. Then it was over and everyone stood in silence, stunned by the dramatic scene they had just witnessed.

***

The heavily bearded, middle-aged man reached up toward the clear blue sky of a perfect day and caught the brown and white Shih Tzu in midair.

"Good job, little friend!" the man said joyfully. Both the man and the dog were ecstatic to be reunited and their love for each other was apparent as the man cuddled the dog and the dog, in turn, wagged its tail furiously.

As always, the man was dressed in a brown rough wool robe with a white rope cincture around his waist. A pair of handmade leather sandals were on his feet. Standing next to him observing the scene was a younger man wearing a white robe that gleamed like the sun. Behind the two of them was a beautiful meadow that bordered a forest bustling with wildlife. In front of them, a clear stream, originating in the hills beyond the meadow, flowed close enough so that one could hear the bubbling sound as it flowed over the rocks in the stream bed.

Surrounding the two, were creatures of many types: deer, foxes, a black wolf, squirrels, other wild creatures and also domestic animals including several horses, sheep and lambs and, of course, dogs, cats and

185

other household pets. A flock of birds sat attentively on the branches of the nearest trees as though waiting for the older man to preach to them as he had in the past. Trout could be seen languishing in pools in the quiet part of the stream. It would be accurate to say it was a heavenly scene.

"Brothers and sisters of the air, brothers and sisters of the land and brothers and sisters of the water," the man named Francis said to his audience. "Let us rejoice that our little brother has returned to us." Then, he petted the Shih Tzu he was holding tenderly and said, "Little fellow, your task is almost completed. There is just one more thing for you to do and you know what it is." He put the dog down on the ground and gently nudged it in the direction of the hills beyond the meadow. The dog gave him a wistful look then turned and ran off to complete his work. Francis looked at the younger man who smiled and nodded his head in approval.

Chapter Twenty-One

There were four of them, all seated at a table in a small, poorly lit and poorly ventilated room in The Palace of the Holy Office, a non-descript building located just south of St. Peter's Basilica inside the Petriano Entrance to Vatican City. Three were cardinals, princes of the Roman Catholic Church and members of the Roman Curia. They were also representatives of the curial Congregation for the Doctrine of the Faith, the Vatican organization that, according to the late Pope John Paul II, is tasked with promoting and safeguarding the doctrine on faith and morals in the whole Catholic world.

The three cardinals were seated on the same side of the table facing the fourth person, Monsignor Enrico Baglio, Chairman of the Pontifical Commission for Supernatural Phenomena. It was a scene reminiscent of the Medieval Inquisition launched by Pope Gregory IX in 1231. No surprise. That very room had been used by the "Inquisitors of Heretical Depravity" several centuries earlier. Fortunately for Monsignor Baglio, those found guilty of deviating from Church doctrine no longer faced torture on the rack.

Cardinal Bernard Kamau of Kenya presided at the hearing and was seated in the middle of the three cardinals. Seated on his left was Cardinal Ottavio Bertotti of Venice and to his right was Cardinal Sean Guin of Seattle. Laying on the table between the three cardinals and the monsignor were a stack of newspapers and a packet of loose photographs. Cardinal Kamau stood up and angrily held up one newspaper after another, each displaying a headline article about Oreo the Miracle Dog.

"It's in every major newspaper all over the world!" the cardinal said sternly. "The New York Times, The Guardian, Sidney Morning Herald, Die Welt, Le Monde, The Asahi Shimbun and even our own L'Osservatore Romano! The dog is getting more coverage than the Trevi earthquake," he sputtered.

Cardinal Bertotti cleared his throat, "It was, of course a touching event. I understand, by the way, that the woman, Stella Righi, will recover from her injuries and that even now she has been reunited with the child and her husband. So, some good has come out of the incident."

"It's not just that incident alone," Cardinal Guin added. "Combined with all of the other incidents, beginning in Hanford, Illinois, and considering the extensive coverage in the news and social media, the animal has become a folk hero."

"More than that!" Cardinal Kamau thundered. "The animal is now seen by hundreds of thousands throughout the world, if not millions, as being a special instrument of the Almighty whose mission is to perform good, selfless works that help people in distress."

"Yes, I find that disturbing, also," Cardinal Bertotti said. "The issue seems to be that people are elevating the dog to the level of a human."

"Agreed," Cardinal Guin said. "There is nothing wrong with recognizing the heroism of a trained dog such as those used by the military or police or for rescue work. However, those animals are just that – animals. They have been trained to respond to certain commands and they do so mindlessly in a Pavlovian manner. There is no rational thought process involved in their actions."

"Monsignor Baglio, was it not your assignment to study the incidents associated with the dog called Oreo and give us a definitive finding regarding the true nature of the animal and its behavior in the context of its mysterious appearances?" Cardinal Kamau asked, bringing the panel's investigation back to the purpose of its current inquiry.

"Yes, of course," the monsignor said.

"Well then, what is the conclusion of the Pontifical Commission for Supernatural Phenomena regarding this matter," Cardinal Kamau challenged.

"It is quite simple, Your Eminence. First, the dog is a dog in all ways that can be observed. Despite our efforts and, we believe, those of at least one foreign government, it was not possible to capture the dog and submit it for ethological analysis. However, there is ample evidence that the physical characteristics and attributes of the animal are those of a canine of the Shih Tzu breed."

"So then, it is simply a dog," Cardinal Guin noted. Monsignor Baglio nodded in agreement.

"Please continue," Cardinal Kamau said.

"Secondly, there was never anything unique about the animal's behavior. By that I mean that it barks like a dog, eats like dog, whines like one and its interaction with humans is much like one would expect from a species of dog that has been bred to be both a watchdog and an affectionate pet – indeed a pet that is often referred to as a lap dog," the monsignor continued.

"However…" Cardinal Bertotti urged.

"However, there is much that is totally unexplainable about the dog and which the members of my Commission and I have concluded are indicative of a supernatural phenomenon – a spiritual one," the monsignor stated.

"Such as," Cardinal Kamau said, his eyes narrowing as though ready to turn the monsignor over to the torturers for his heresy.

The monsignor hesitated for a moment and then said, "The dog could not possibly have traveled the considerable distances from incident location to incident location without external intervention. Further, we believe it is impossible that the dog could have appeared exactly when needed to impact a human situation by providing comfort, solace or encouragement or, in the most recent case where the dog clearly saved a child from certain death, in the absence of divine intervention. In addition, there have been many similarly reported non-human incidents where the dog saved other animals from one fate or another. Again, the travel factor defies explanation."

The room was filled with silence. Cardinal Bertotti made notes on a legal pad he brought with him while the other two cardinals sat back in their chairs and pondered the monsignor's verbal report.

"In other words, your commission believes that the dog's behavior was divinely directed and that he acted in shall we say a saintly manner," Cardinal Bertotti quipped.

"An animal saint," Cardinal Kamau said disparagingly. "Can you imagine what nonsense that is. However, that's what some of them out there want, you know. There are petitions arising everywhere for the Church to make the creature a saint. Bah!"

"It would not be the first time that an animal was made a saint," Monsignor Baglio added.

The three cardinals stared at the monsignor menacingly. "What are you talking about?" Cardinal Guin asked before a vague recollection of a historical event filtered into his memory.

"I am speaking about St. Guinefort, a rather heroic Greyhound of the 12th Century," the monsignor said in a matter-of-fact tone.

All three cardinals jumped to their feet, a look of disbelief on their faces.

"Heresy!" shouted Cardinal Kamau.

"Preposterous!" Cardinal Bertotti screamed.

"Not fair," Cardinal Guin said, more calmly. "Guinefort was never actually canonized by the Church."

"Neither were the vast majority of those who are acknowledged saints in the eyes of the Church," Monsignor Baglio countered. "The first person canonized by a Pope was Ulrich, Bishop of Augsburg who died in 973 and was canonized by Pope John XV in 993. Until that time, people were proclaimed saints by acclamation of local cults or the local bishop. St. Patrick of Ireland is one example. He was never canonized," Monsignor Baglio reminded his ecclesiastical superiors.

"Don't lecture us, monsignor" Cardinal Bertotti said angrily. We know that. However, who or what is this St. Guinefort you are talking about.?"

"As you might recall, Your Eminences," the monsignor said somewhat condescendingly, "According to a 13th Century Dominican Friar, Stephen of Bourbon, Guinefort was a Greyhound owned by a wealthy knight in the Dombes region of France, near Lyon. One day the knight and his wife left their baby son in the care of a nursemaid and their dog, Guinefort. When they returned, the nursemaid was nowhere to be found. The nursery was in shambles and covered with blood, as was the muzzle of the dog, who seemed to have been injured.

"The knight thought the dog had killed the baby. He drew his sword and in a rage killed the animal. Moments later, he discovered the baby alive and well, sleeping safely elsewhere in the room. The knight also discovered the mutilated body of a large snake and belatedly concluded that the dog had defended the child preventing the snake from killing it."

Two of the three cardinals stood silently, mesmerized by the story. However, Cardinal Guin sat down and put a hand to his head knowing what the monsignor would say next.

"Realizing he had unjustly killed the dog Guinefort, the knight buried the animal outside of his castle and erected a small monument to his bravery," the monsignor continued. "However, the local peasants who

192

heard the story proclaimed the dog a martyr whose soul was surely in heaven. They began bringing their sick babies to the dog's burial site in hope that the dog would intervene with the Lord on their behalf and the children would be cured. Many were cured and, according to folklore, a cult soon developed. It was not long before Guinefort was proclaimed a saint by local acclamation."

Perplexed, the other two cardinals sat down in their chairs. "Yes, now that you have so kindly refreshed our minds, I do recall the tale," Cardinal Kamau said.

"We should recall it," Cardinal Bertotti added. "In fact, despite many attempts to eradicate the cult and its misguided veneration of the dog, it continued well into the early part of the past century."

"So, what is your point, monsignor? I think we can all agree that only a human can legitimately be called a saint," Cardinal Kamau inquired.

"Really?" Monsignor Baglio said. "Are angels humans?"

"Of course not!" Cardinal Guin retorted.

"Then how is it that the title Saint has been given to Saint Michael the Archangel, Saint Gabriel the Archangel and Saint Raphael the Archangel, to name only a few non-humans whom we also call saints?" the monsignor concluded.

Cardinal Kamau crossed himself and sternly said, "Enough!" He looked at his watch. "It is almost 10:00 am. His Holiness is due for his weekly general audience in St. Peter's Square in a half hour and all of us must attend. We will reconvene tomorrow at the same time."

With that, he and the other cardinals abruptly stood up and left the room. Monsignor Baglio took out a handkerchief and wiped the growing perspiration from his brow. The worst was likely to come the following morning he thought. "Beh, why me?" he wondered in his native Italian.

Chapter Twenty-Two

As usual, St. Peter's Square was filled to capacity as the faithful, and the curious, lined up to see the pope and hear his brief remarks. A circular path had been cleared around the square where the pope would ride the popemobile as he waved to the crowd and gave them his blessing. Immediately outside the basilica, a large platform had been erected where the pope and dignitaries, such as members of the Curia, would sit and from which the pope would make his address.

All proceeded as usual – at first. Then, as the pope rode in the back of the popemobile, he began noticing signs that were held up with slogans like:

Canonize Oreo

Oreo the Miracle Dog

Oreo, the Trevi Martyr

Saint Oreo

Oreo, a Gift from God

The pope turned to one of the men riding in the back seat of the vehicle – actually a member of the Swiss Guard who was guarding him – and asked what the signs were all about. The man whispered something to the pope who simply smiled and continued to wave to the crowd. However, when the audience was completed, the pope asked Monsignor Cotnoir, Prefect of the Papal Household and the Holy Father's personal assistant, what prompted the signs. Monsignor Cotnoir briefed the pope, who seldom read a newspaper or watched television, about the attention being given throughout the world's press and news media to the events surrounding the unexplained appearances and interventions of a dog named Oreo. After hearing the explanation, The pope told the monsignor that he wanted to speak with Cardinal Florio, who was the highest ranking cardinal on the Roman Curia.

***

At 9:00 am the following morning, the three cardinals and Monsignor Baglio were once again assembled in the inquisitorial room in the Palace of the Holy Office. Cardinal Kamau opened the meeting on a less confrontational note than the one on which the previous meeting ended.

"So, Monsignor Baglio, the conclusion of your Commission is what?" the cardinal asked.

"We believe that the dog may have been sent to us as a messenger," he said.

"A messenger," Cardinal Guin restated. The monsignor nodded. "About what?" Cardinal Guin asked.

Monsignor Baglio opened a thin, black portfolio briefcase and pulled out four sets of photographs. He kept one for himself and gave each of the cardinals a set.

"These are photos of a mural in the chapel of St. Francis of Assisi in the Church of Our Lady of Tears in Trevi," he said. The three cardinals studied the photos intently. "May I ask, Your Eminences, what you see in the photos."

"Obviously, the figure in the brown robe and sandals is supposed to be St. Francis," Cardinal Bertotti said.

"It is a mural of nature," Cardinal Kamau opined. "It is a beautiful pastoral scene with St. Francis, many different types of animals, trees, hills in the background and a gentle stream running through all if it."

"Good grief!" exclaimed Cardinal Guin. "There are two dogs running around playfully near St. Francis. One of them is unmistakably a Greyhound and the other is..." he stopped short as he looked up at Monsignor Baglio.

"A little brown and white Shih Tzu with floppy ears and a fluffy tail," the monsignor said as he finished the cardinal's sentence for him.

"I don't understand," said Cardinal Kamau.

"St. Francis is known for his love of nature and of animals," the monsignor said. "But most of all, he was known for helping those who were suffering and those in need. We think that the message we are being sent is that we must take better care of our neighbor, whether homeless or immigrant or ill or in danger and we must better respect our precious endangered environment."

The three cardinals sat in silence pondering Monsignor Baglio's words. Cardinal Guin was the first to speak, "I cannot get over the two dogs in the mural," he said. "They are almost certainly Oreo and Guinefort. When was the mural painted?"

"Several hundred years ago. The story of Guinefort would likely have been known by then, but no one of that time could possibly have known about the exploits of the Shih Tzu," the monsignor said.

There was a collective sigh among the cardinals. Then Cardinal Kamau asked, "What does your commission propose? Even if we could agree that the dog was sent to us as a sign or messenger, as you suggest, we could not possibly allow the animal to be venerated."

"Certainly not as a human holy person or saint might be," the monsignor agreed. "However, we also have to recognize that in the case of St. Guinefort, that cult persisted for hundreds of years."

"You want us to allow the dog to be called a saint, then?" Cardinal Bertotti said.

"A folklore saint, if you will," replied the monsignor. "Look, according to doctrine, any soul going to heaven is a saint, whether proclaimed or not."

"But, Guinefort notwithstanding, surely not the soul of an animal," Cardinal Guin suggested.

"Why not," the monsignor asked. "Our current Holy Father's predecessor, Pope Francis, was not only a great supporter of protecting the environment, but he also publically opined that all animals have souls, albeit not like human souls, and that they are welcome in heaven."

Returning to a business-like mode, Cardinal Kamau stood and said, "Monsignor Baglio, speaking for myself and my cardinals, we appreciate the work that you and your commission have done and we will take your suggestions under advisement. This inquiry is now adjourned. Oh, one more thing, monsignor. His Holiness wants to you to join him for breakfast tomorrow."

Chapter Twenty-Three

They sat together in the papal apartment like old friends enjoying a weekly breakfast together. In fact, they had known each other since seminary days when they were simply Enrico Baglio and Pietro Moretti. Then time passed and each walked a different path. Enrico Baglio was content to be a parish priest who had not the slightest ambition to advance within the hierarchy of the Church. Pietro Moretti pursued a difference course that eventually saw him become a bishop and then a cardinal.

Then one day, His Eminence Pietro Moretti found himself sequestered in the Sistine Chapel with the other princes of the Church. Sadly, they were electing a successor to the cardinal's mentor, Pope Francis, whose weakened remaining lung no longer permitted him to perform the strenuous duties of the Holy Office. A ballot was cast and much to his dismay, because it was the last thing he wanted, when ballots were counted white smoke rose from the small chimney on the roof of the chapel and Pietro Moretti was proclaimed Pope Pius XIII.

Although Monsignor Baglio sensed what the pope had on his mind, he relaxed the best he could and enjoyed breakfast. There was much small talk as the two men chatted about the challenges facing the Church and the changing moral values of society. After breakfast had been completed, the pope changed the subject and said, "Enrico, Kamau tells me that there is something you would like me to read."

The monsignor nodded, retrieved his portfolio from a nearby table and opened it. He reached inside and took out a two-page document, handing it to the pontiff. The pope read it carefully then handed it back to the monsignor.

"You know, Enrico, His Holiness Pope Francis was both a mentor and a very good friend to me. One day, our conversation turned to the subject of whether or not animals, like domestic pets, have souls and if so whether they go to heaven when they die. Pope Francis's position was that they did have souls, not like human souls, but ones that survived death. He further believed that animals by their nature do not need redemption like we humans do. Therefore, when an animal dies its soul goes directly to heaven. He asked me what my views were on the subject."

The pope got up from the table at which they were seated and got three glasses of different sizes from a cabinet and put them on the table. One was a small juice glass. Another was a wine glass and the third was a large water tumbler. He took a water pitcher and filled all three glasses.

"I strongly disagreed with His Holiness," the Pope continued. "Then he got up from the table at which we were seated in this very apartment and took out these same glasses."

The monsignor had a blank look on his face. He had no idea what the purpose of the glasses and water were. The pope continued,

"Pope Francis asked me which of the three glasses was filled. I said that all three were, of course. They were all filled to their capacity. Then he said, 'And so it is with souls in heaven. The large glass represents the soul of an angel, a higher level being than a human. The wine glass represents the human soul and the small juice glass represents the soul of an animal. Each soul has a certain capacity for fulfillment and in heaven each one is fulfilled.' I thought about what that good man said and ever since I have had a different perspective about an animal's role in God's creation."

Monsignor Baglio did not know what to say. He thought that the pope might be suggesting he was open to the proposed document he had given him earlier to read. But, he could not be sure. Then, the pope said, "Enrico, that bacon gave me a little *agida*, indigestion. Let's take a walk in the garden."

The Vatican Gardens are among the most beautiful in the world. Spread over forty acres, the perfectly manicured gardens are lush with palms, exotic trees, flower beds, topiaries, green lawns and even a four-acre forest. For his walk, the pope chose the French Garden because of its colorful flower beds and conveniently located benches where he could stop and rest. The two men walked a while in silence. Then, the pope pointed to a bench overlooking a broad stretch of flower beds redundant with color.

They sat on the bench for a few minutes enjoying the view. Then the pope said, "Enrico, my friend, I share my predecessor's feelings about the environment and about animals. However, what you and your commission propose simply cannot be. Animals have a special place in

God's creation just like humans and angels do. However, animals simply cannot become saints."

"We are not proposing they be considered saints in the same sense that humans are, Holy Father. However, the one called Oreo clearly has a special place in creation and we simply propose that you allow him to take his place in folklore and be accorded whatever title the people choose for him. The Church does not need to formally recognize or endorse whatever title that might be."

"Let me see that paper again, Enrico," the Pope said. The monsignor pulled it from the portfolio and gave the two-page document to the pope. "I see that you title it an Apostolic Brief, which is simply a document dealing with a matter of minor importance. That's good."

"Yes, Holy Father. We believe that is all that is necessary to satisfy the mass of people who want to see some special status for the dog."

"Still, the term saint, even if used in a folklore sense, implies much more. I am sorry, Enrico. I cannot put my signature on the brief. I am afraid it would take a special message from the Lord to persuade me to sign ..." The pope's thoughts were interrupted by something he spotted happening at the far end of the garden.

"What's going on over there, Enrico?"

"I don't know, Your Holiness. I think it's just Armando the gardener working."

"It looks like he is chasing something," the pope said. "A rabbit maybe. No, it's a little dog."

"Yes, it is a dog, Holy Father, and it's running this way. Armando is chasing it."

The pope looked at the monsignor. "It's a little brown and white dog, Enrico," he observed, his voice carrying the tone of inevitability. "Cute, isn't he?"

With Armando the gardener in hot pursuit, the dog slowed down from a run and sat right in front of the pope and the monsignor. It's tail was wagging furiously. Two tags hung from a blue collar around its neck and it carried something in its mouth. Monsignor Baglio squinted as he tried to read the tags.

"Don't bother, Enrico," the Pope sighed. "I think we both know what they are." He looked down at the dog and asked, "What do you have in your mouth, Oreo? What are you bringing me?"

The monsignor bent over, gently took the object from the dog's mouth and handed it to the Pope. "It's a pen, Your Holiness, one of your papal pens."

Saint Oreo

About the Author

Louis E. Tagliaferri is a retired management consultant, publisher, and author. During his career, he wrote many business educational works including seven non-fiction books. After his retirement, Lou's writing interests turned to fiction where he first authored a series of three novels based on the lives of his and his wife Judy's European immigrant grandparents: *Bellaria di Rivergaro, The Web Shop* and *The Habsburg Cowboys*. He then authored a series of three historical fiction novels focusing on the Spanish Colonial and pioneer period in Florida and the southeast states: *In Search of Becca and The Virgin of Tears, The Timucuan* and *Cracker Landing*. His most recent novel, *Saint Oreo, The Miracle Dog* is a total departure from his earlier themes and will appeal to anyone looking for a fun and uplifting story. Lou lives in Ponte Vedra Beach, Florida with Judy, his wife of over 60 years. In addition to writing works of fiction and non-fiction, he has enjoyed sailing, flying general aviation aircraft, playing golf and, of course, the family's little Shih Tzu, Oreo.

Saint Oreo

The Real Oreo

Saint Oreo

Saint Oreo

76094662R00120

Made in the USA
Columbia, SC
24 September 2019